# Heaven's Eyes

Jacqueline J. Andrews

# Dedication....

I dedicate this book to some special people, who are gone but not forgotten and on whose shoulders I stand.

My maternal grandparents: Amos Doyle and Sadie Mae Doyle

My father: Ula T. Jennings

Your love continues in me...

I also dedicate this book to my wonderful mother: Mary Jennings

Jacqueline J. Andrews
*Heaven's Eyes*

# 1

*Heaven knows/*
*omniscient wide eyes that watch the world*
*in its candor and in its grief.*
*In the murky darkness/*
*in the force of daylight*
*the sky never slumbers or sleeps.*

Annie Moss remembered her great-grandmother saying, "Heaven knows," when she was a child, a "wee lil thang" as her great-grandmother had often referred to her. She wondered now if Heaven still knew – if it cared about her losses, her small victories, her offspring.

She sat on the porch of the old wooden house rocking back and forth in her chair, her eyes closed. She listened as her great-grandchildren played games in the yard, spinning around and around in a circle, their voices blending to form a sound that was as sweet music to her ears. She smiled, lifting her head trying to focus on the kaleidoscope of colors – the deep green grass, the radiant four o'clock flowers budding in the afternoon sun, and the mixture of little brown faces. She huffed, cursing her failing eyesight. So many years had passed, yet the remnants of those days still danced about in her consciousness.

At age 85, Annie felt at peace. Her years on earth had been filled and her time had come – her course was finished. As she sat there rocking, her mind drifted back to the day her sister Linda had come back to Macklin, Mississippi.

Annie was a young woman of 19, and she and Henry had been married a year. They had hopes of a prosperous future together in spite of the nay sayers in town. Even amidst her newfound excitement as a young bride, as always, she had thought of Heaven watching.

\*    \*    \*

## 1939

Clouds danced in rapid formation, mingling ever so gently without making a sound. Moisture was in the air – hot and sweet like a garden in the evening sun. It was not to be an ordinary day Annie thought, as she peeked out the window of the house. Henry and the baby hadn't stirred when she got out of bed at 6:30 over an hour before.

She fanned her face with her hand, as she thought about how hot she was already and it wasn't even 8a.m. yet. Busy with her morning chores, she hurried back to the bedroom and watched Henry sleep – his breathing steady and quiet. She often wondered how he slept so soundly, while she snored like a freight train.

"Henry, you…"

"I'm up, I'm up. I knew you was comin' in here, so I'm already up."

"Well if you knowed it, you ought'a been up and out that bed! You got plenty to do around here. My sister don't float into town every day."

"Alright woman, you don't have to shout so all of Macklin can hear you, I'm movin.'"

Henry got out of bed, mumbling as Annie gathered up the sheets preparing them for the laundry. Her mother had always told her that men are just like children; you have to keep them in line lest they stray away too far.

Annie began putting new sheets on the bed and sighed as she remembered the first time she saw Henry. Even then she knew that he was the one for her. The twinkle in her eyes gave her away as her mother pulled her along telling her, *Don't even thank about it missy. That boy gat a track record so long, you can jump rope wid it. Gat it honest too, 'cuz his daddy'll snuggle up to anything that moves!*

Earlene's words went in one ear and out of the other it seemed, and before Annie knew it, Henry was courting her and winning her heart.

*     *     *

The baby startled Annie as she fumbled with the sheets on the bed. Hester wriggled her tiny arms about in her basinet. It was the fanciest thing Annie had ever seen. *Nothing but the best for our first born*, she told Henry that day at Pike's General Store. She fixed it up with a quilt and pillows that her mother had handmade. Annie knew that she would get good use out of it for years to come.

Annie picked the baby up and put her on her shoulder as she walked to the kitchen.

"That lil' angel done woke up?"

"Yeah, she got up fussin' this morning again." Annie bounced Hester, soothing her some.

"Well, I guess I'll get started." Henry headed out to the coop to feed the chickens.

Annie slowly sat down, and she and Hester stared into each other's eyes. The world seemed to melt away as she nursed her. She thought about Linda coming back to

Macklin. It had been two years since she had left for Chicago, only to return with nothing but shattered hope and a broken heart with bruises to boot. Linda had written Annie all about it, and now she was coming back home for a fresh start.

Macklin wasn't so bad, Annie thought. After all, it was all she knew. There were things about it that she loved and things about it that made her ashamed. It was a close community; sometimes a little too close, and yet distanced enough for everyone to pretend that they didn't know everyone else's business. There was the time when Earlene had told Annie and Linda that their neighbor, Virginia, had "broke her leg," which meant she was pregnant. Of course when Earlene spoke to Virginia's mother in Pike's, Earlene pretended to be astonished to hear the news.

Henry scattered the chicken feed around the yard, his mind wandering. He remembered the scandals that Linda and Dyson McCloud had stirred up, and not to mention a few other men.

"Henry?" Annie ran out of the back door, catching up to Henry.

"What is it sugar?"

"Linda's train gone be comin' round noon, and you still gotta go over to Dyson's to pick up that chest for me."

"There's plenty time Annie. I'll make it there on time."

"Well, make sho you do because I'm'a cook Linda's favorite supper tonight – some black eyed peas, fried chicken, and a jelly cake for dessert."

"You sho glad for Linda comin ain't you?"

"She *is* my only sister. I missed her when she was off in Chicago." Annie began staring off into space.

"Where she stayin?" Henry asked more out of curiosity than concern.

"With mama and daddy for a while I guess, but I reckon she wouldn't wanna stay there too long." She followed Henry's every move while he worked. Shielding the sun with her hand, she tried to focus on Henry as he pumped water from the well.

Henry filled the last bucket and took the rag from his pocket to wipe his brow.

"Maybe she can stay in that lil place over yonder there." Henry pointed across the yard to a small shack sitting idle. "It's run down some now, but me and Dyson can have it fixed up in no time."

Annie's eyes scanned the distance across the yard. "That place?"

"I don't see why not – if she wants to that is."

"Well, maybe she just might for a while. I would love to have her close to me. She can help out with the babies." Annie rubbed her stomach and smiled.

"Yeah, she gon' love lil' Hester." Henry chuckled, not noticing Annie's last gesture.

Annie walked toward Henry after looking back at Hester in her basket on the kitchen table. "She gon' love both our babies Henry."

"You mean…"

"That's right Henry, you gon' be a daddy, again."

Henry picked Annie up, spinning her around, and kissed her hard on the lips.

"You know I love you more than anything."

Annie looked up toward Henry, his very presence sending shocks through her body. She adored all six feet two inches of his chocolate frame. The way his skin looked next to her ivory complexion was amazing to her still. He towered over her tiny five-foot frame, and she reveled in how comfortable she felt knowing that Henry would always be there to love and protect her.

# 2

Linda twitched in her seat, fidgeting like a nervous child before a beating. She couldn't decide whether to feel relieved about going back to Macklin or just plain sad. She wrestled about going back home having to explain why she was back when she said that Macklin would be a distant memory. She knew the folks in Macklin would be trying to pry as sure as her name was Linda Bernice Rankin. But at least she was coming back with a new last name. Not that she had anything to show for it except Eddie Rankin's tracks up and down her back.

Linda thought that her life was finally heading for some kind of success, at least something separate from the country living she had always known. After just a few short months after she left Macklin, she found herself living in a big city with a handsome man and a fancy apartment to boot. Then she found out that Eddie was still married to his "first" wife, and it went downhill from there. Early one morning, Eddie's wife came walking through the door – had caught Linda and Eddie right in the act.

Eddie was suspended in a moment that his brain couldn't register. Linda was underneath his sweaty body, and his wife was standing in the doorway. He had wanted to complete his climax, but his wife, Vicki, interrupted the dance and insisted on cutting in.

There was something that Linda could never understand. She would often ask herself why a man feels like he has to lie and sneak around just to get a woman. If he was half the man he thought he was, he should know that a woman will take him wrapped up just as he is. Linda felt that women were different that way.

As her legs shifted in her seat, Linda remembered her mother Earlene saying, *Ain't no use in cryin' over spilt milk – just wipe it up and pour some more honey.* When Linda thought of her mother, she thought that she loved her as much as she could, even though Earlene had made a difference between her light and dark daughters. Her sister Annie was a yellow little thing from the time she tumbled out of Earlene's womb. Everybody loved Annie. She also remembered that Annie was her mama and daddy's pride and joy.

Still and all, she couldn't say that Annie or her mother was the reason she left Macklin. She knew that it was something bigger than the dysfunction in her family that made her leave the south. Light skin, dark skin. White – Black. Bright/Dark. It all just made her want something different. Linda hated her chocolate skin all her life. It couldn't be helped in a town like Macklin, but in Chicago, she had felt like she was painted in black gold the way people looked at her. "Pretty to be dark" was how her mama described her to most folks. But Linda's personal philosophy was that a girl should always think she's pretty, and a *woman* should *know* it.

That was one thing she loved about Eddie – he went crazy over her. "Love at first sight" he had claimed. She went wild over him too. She thought that it seemed like it was always the ones who looked like Eddie who wasn't worth two cents. He was tall with striking features and green eyes a girl could fall into. He also had a talent for loving a woman so good her knees would buckle.

As she rode along on that train, nodding in and out of consciousness, she vowed to put it all behind her. She had to think about what was ahead of her.

Going back to Macklin was just as good a start as any. Annie had written her about her marriage to Henry and her new baby girl, Hester. Though Linda thought that Henry Moss was just like the rest of his brothers, she didn't reveal it to Annie in the letter she had written to her. Linda felt that Henry had stuck his Willie in just one woman too many, just like his daddy and the rest of his brothers. She also knew that Earlene tried to tell Annie that, but when a girl is in love, her head is like sheet rock. She just thought that maybe Annie was able to straighten him out – a girl like her just might be able to do it.

Earlene had always preached that Henry Moss was just like his daddy and brothers. Nothing but high yellow women would satisfy them. She would go on to say that it was some nerve they had, *seeing how all them Moss men were just as black as night*. Still and all, Linda thought that Annie was one lucky girl, being married with a child, even if it was just old Henry Moss.

Annie was always a good girl and had never been with nobody else but Henry. Linda had made her way around town and back again. She knew that if nobody else would be, most of the men in Macklin would be glad to see her. Dyson McCloud was one of them. He wanted to marry Linda at one time, but her mother said he was too old. Linda felt that it was because he wasn't perfect. To Linda, Earlene had a thing about perfection that she could never understand. She thought that it was because deep down, her mother knew that she had imperfections of her own.

Dyson only has three fingers on his left hand. He lost the other two when he was a boy. Some say a plow ran over his hand. Others say his father chopped them off for stealing. The legend of Dyson's lost fingers had announced itself in countless ways around Macklin.

Dyson wasn't considered a handsome man, but he had plenty of money. His daddy died and left him a big house and a lot of land. She remembered that Dyson would buy her anything she asked for. Even though his wife had been gone a whole year when Linda started seeing Dyson, those nosy biddies in town still called her a home wrecker. So she left – regretting a little that she had to give up that kind of attention from a man, but she wasn't taking any chances. She couldn't say that she was in love with Dyson, but she knew, however, that she wouldn't have had to work for the rest of her days.

Nobody else back home ever really caught her eye except those Moss boys. Henry's brother, David, was chasing what was under her dress for a while - only problem was, his wife wouldn't let him catch the prize. So the only thing left for Linda to do was to leave Macklin, start over, and make something of herself. Or better still, marry a man who had already done so.

The closer the train got to the station, the more circles Linda's stomach turned. She hated to go back to living with her folks. Ever since Annie had written that her great-grandmother was living with Earlene and Jeb now, Linda knew that there would be two old meddling hens in her business now instead of one. Her great-grandmother always seemed to know things before they happened. Linda remembered her saying, "Heaven knows, and tells me all of its secrets."

Looking out of the window reminded her of all the reasons she left Macklin.  There was no excitement, no bright lights – just grass and trees and more trees.  She prayed that she wouldn't suffocate when she got off the train.  Right away, she knew that she didn't miss the Mississippi heat – her new hairdo was not up for the damp air.  It was a good thing she was wearing her hat straight from Marshall Fields.

At least she was proud of her wardrobe to show off from her high living as Mrs. Eddie Rankin.  Lord knew she didn't get anything else.

At last there it was – Macklin Station.  And standing there waiting to pick her up was her brother-in-law, Henry Moss.  As far as Linda was concerned, her life could begin again.

# 3

The station wasn't crowded for a Friday afternoon, but then there were never really too many visitors in Macklin, and people rarely left. Linda stepped off the train with a suitcase and two hat boxes that seemed to be carrying her. Her slight stumble sent Henry rushing over to rescue her.

"Let me help you with that Linda. How was the ride?"

"Just fine Henry. Just fine. Can't say I'm doing too well, but it feels kind of good to be home – for the moment anyway." She lied.

Henry wiped at his brow with his hand, ignoring the rag in his back pocket. As they walked over to the car, they spotted Ms. Erma and Odessa Phillips walking out of Pike's General Store. The two of them had been lifelong friends, even through the death of their husbands. They spent the rest of their lives as Linda's mother Earlene Hicks put it, *Talkin bout their children, their grandchildren, and anything else gat legs.*

They looked over toward Henry and Linda and waved politely, disguised in their forced trademark smiles.

"Ah see that frolickin' floozy done found her way back to town." Ms. Erma spat to Odessa through the side of her mouth while still smiling.

"Mm hmm, just like a wayward dog." Odessa replied, just before yelling over to Linda.

"Welcome back sugar – it's so good to see ya!"

"Likewise Ms. Odessa," Linda yelled, hardly fooled by the smiling faces.

She whispered to Henry still smiling.

"Those two biddies still gossipin about everything they see?"

"Mm, hmm." Henry said chuckling. "*And* everything they don't!" The two of them laughed as they climbed into the car.

The ride was smooth to Henry and Annie's farm. Linda took in everything she had left two years before. The smell of honeysuckle tickled her nose, and her eyes admired the beauty of outstretched land. She fanned herself with her hand as she studied the landscape; the giant trees that stretched across the infinite fields of green; the tiny houses that stood on blocks, placed sparingly throughout the wide open spaces. They passed the dairy farm owned by Mr. Dale Hinckley, a stout, blush-faced white man. His family had been in Macklin County long before the Civil War.

The rumor around town about the Hinckley family was that Dale's mother had married her first cousin. Earlene had told Annie and Linda that Dale was teased for his funny looks back when they were children because of it. Linda sighed, as she remembered that story and the many others that came from Earlene. She looked around inside the car.

"I guess Annie's a lucky girl. She get to ride in a fancy car like this anytime she like." Linda ran her hand over the vinyl seat.

"Yeah, daddy gave it to me when Annie and me got married. Second best weddin' present I got."

"My husband had a car too." Linda stared into space. "And he was a good driver, livin in a big city like Chicago and all." She said it proudly. She then thought about how silly she must have sounded and removed the smile from her lips.

Henry kept his eyes on the road, his nostrils soaking up the hint of Linda's perfume; the smell of damp Jasmine.

"Yeah, city drivin ain't for everybody I reckon. This here's all I'll ever need."

Annie came running out of the door with Hester in her arms.

"Linny!" She screamed almost tripping as she approached the still moving car.

Linda hopped out of the car as soon as it stopped.

"Ain't this something? Married with a baby and still can't call my name right." She threw her arms around Annie.

"I know how to say it *Linda*, but I still likes to remember the old times. This is Hester." She handed her to Linda.

"Awe, she just as sweet as pumpkin pie." Linda swept Hester up in her arms, kissing her and twirling her about. "I love her already!"

Hester was the image of Annie. She had skin the color of alabaster with eyes like cinnamon. Her hair was thick and curly, which made her grandmother, Earlene, proud. Earlene would often say, "I pray God that Annie's children look just like her when they come here."

Linda flinched as she remembered her mother's prediction of Annie having *bright* babies.

As the three of them walked toward the door of the house, Henry watched the sisters as they laughed and reminisced.

"Come on in this house girl. I done fixed your favorite supper."

"I sho hope it's fried chicken and black-eyed-peas." Linda licked her lips and closed her eyes for a split second.

"Well you won't find out walkin slow as you is. Come on girl!"

*     *     *

"So tell me about that big ole city of Chicago." Annie looked at Linda with excitement in her voice. Linda was helping her with the dishes, and Henry was in the front room rocking Hester and singing her to sleep.

Linda slid some suds from her hands and dried them on the dishrag. She pulled a chair from the table, sat down, and cleared her throat.

"Well, let's see Annie. It was everything I dreamed it would be. There were tall fancy buildings and busy streets. I could have caught a slew of flies in my mouth the whole first week I was there cause I walked around with it hanging open so much. Me and a few girls that I met on the train ride there roomed together in a little place off of Madison Street. We was all looking for something other than what we knew I suppose." Linda gazed off into nowhere.

"Did you really get the money for the train ride, doing… what Ms. Erma said you did?" Annie asked quietly, looking into her sister's eyes.

"I got the money from Dyson if it's anybody's business." Linda stood abruptly from the table. "Ms. Erma just mad cause I didn't want that low down son James of hers that's all."

"Linda I didn't mean…"

"I know Annie," Linda sat down again. "It's just that I know what people said about me when I left Macklin, and I don't care no more. I'm back here and there ain't nothing nobody can do about it." Linda looked down at her hands.

The sight of them took her briefly to another place in time. "I had a beautiful ring from Eddie, but I sold it to get back here."

The two of them talked for hours. Linda told Annie about Chicago and how she met Eddie Rankin. He was a saxophone player who played the blues with some of the best. She also told her about the big names that Eddie dropped to her. She had no clue as to who they were, but she guessed them to be important. Still, she bragged about them to any and everybody.

"He said he knew Alberta Hunter, Charles "Cow-Cow" Davenport, and Blind Lemon Jefferson. All he talked about was that music of his. I met him one night at a little place called the Blue Room. Me and my friends went there after work one night and he was there. After putting in 10 hours a day at the hotel, we couldn't wait to go to that place and dance our tails off! Yeah... that's where I met Eddie."

\*       \*       \*

Eddie "Rib-Eye" Rankin was a small-time talent from Baton Rouge, Louisiana. His friends gave him the nickname "Rib-Eye" because he could play the saxophone so well, it could make your ears tingle and your mouth water. He'd been playing ever since he was six years old. His grandfather played the banjo on a plantation, his father the saxophone. And just like a little boy who dreams of walking in his father's shoes, Eddie picked up the sax and had never put it down.

Eddie was the color of butter and had eyes like deep set emeralds. He could attract just about any woman he wanted with his looks alone, but coupled with his talent as a musician, he was irresistible to women of every creed and color. Coming to Chicago was a must for him, according to his friend, Al Jeter. Al had said that Eddie's life would not be the same. Chicago had a zest of life to offer much more than the south ever would.

Al played the piano and was one of the best musicians around. He'd told Eddie about the Blue Room. The next thing Eddie knew, the four of them, Al, Eddie, and their wives, were on a train heading to the bright lights of Chicago. Both men were married, but they would often let their eyes wander and their bodies would always follow.

Eddie had only been in town all of two weeks. His wife Vicki was a dancer that he'd met back in Louisiana. Shortly after they arrived in Chicago, she had sailed to Paris to pursue her dance career, leaving Eddie to his own devices. One such device would soon appear in the form of a mocha colored, hip sashaying hotel maid named Linda Hicks.

# 4

As the evening sun set on the house, Earlene paced around the kitchen as she set the table for supper. Having already raised her daughters, Linda and Annie, she was now taking care of her elderly grandmother. It was no small feat, for Ruthann was a no-nonsense 90 year-old woman who was not of few words. She often gave her opinion on just about any matter, whether anyone asked for it or not. Earlene's children revered her as their only living grandparent, and at the same time feared her. Earlene's husband, Jeb, attempted to steer clear of Ruthann's wrath whenever he could.

Jeb felt as if nothing he ever did for Earlene was good enough for her grandmother, Ms. Ruthann. He told anyone who would listen that Ruthann must have her ear glued to their bedroom door at night because she knew about every little tiff that he and Earlene had.

"Mama! Jeb! Yall come on in here now, supper's ready." Earlene called into the parlor as she pulled a chair from the table.

Ruthann shuffled into the kitchen on her cane. Her husband had been gone now for two years. She would often walk around the house, mumbling to herself. Every now and then, Earlene could swear that Ruthann was still talking to her late husband.

"Ah'm coming chile!" Ruthann snapped. "You ain't got to yell it. Ah hope you done fixed somethin' nuther that ah can digest this time. Lord knows that sausage of yourn from this morning *still* rumbling around in my belly." She eased a chair from the table as Jeb came running over.

"Let me get that for you Ms. Ruthann." Jeb pulled the chair back and helped her to her seat.

"Thank you baby. Ah guess you still got some manners left in you, but…"

"But it's time to eat." Earlene cut her off before she could start in on Jeb. "Honey, please say the grace." Earlene almost pleaded to Jeb.

The first few minutes of a meal was always quiet at the Hicks' table. There was always tension between Jeb and Ruthann, and Earlene, without fail awaited her grandmother's next remark.

"So I hear that Linda done made it back to town." Jeb chewed his fried corn, breaking the silence.

"Yeah, Ms. Odessa told me her train came in this afternoon." Earlene sat her iced tea down. She's over to Annie and Henry's place now. Can't wait to see my baby."

"Ah don't know what kind of chile wouldn't come see her mama and daddy fore she up and go someplace else." Ruthann chimed in, getting up from the table.

"Mama where you goin?" Earlene asked, although she knew what she would hear next.

"Ah'm goin back in here to sat a while and rest my mouth so ah can chew this here chicken." She arose from the chair, and turned to Jeb. "And don't bother me none 'cause I can make it by myself."

She got to the doorway of the kitchen, her eyes narrowed as she turned and spoke. "Ah love my granddawta, but Heaven knows it ain't gonna be long 'fore Linda stirs up somethin nuther round here." Ruthann turned back around and walked away mumbling to no one in particular. "Ah still can't go into town without somebody talking about her and Dyson."

Earlene rolled her eyes upward. "Mama I don't know why you still talking about that. It's over and done with."

"And the only people who still talking about it, are the ones who made up the lies in the first place." Jeb intervened, directing his voice toward the parlor.

"Honey, not now." Earlene waived her hand at Jeb. "Let's just finish supper in peace."

The two of them continued eating and chatted about Linda while pausing between the light snores from the parlor. The dog was doing his ritualistic evening scratch at the back door. The sun was giving its final bow, and the breeze whistled through the screen door. All was finally quiet in the Hicks household again… for now.

# 5

     Dyson lifted his head from the pillow. He slowly opened his eyes and focused on the room. The sweltering heat had awakened him again. His nights seemed to get longer, especially after Linda left town. The gin his constant companion, the morning light his archenemy. He climbed out of bed quickly succumbing to his sacrament of scratching himself, then stretching his arms far and wide. His feet hit the floor and led him to the kitchen to soothe his dry throat.

     He grabbed a tin cup from the icebox and tilted it back quick and hard to his mouth. He gave a slight grunt as the alcohol stung his throat. He shook his head and wiped his mouth with his mangled hand. His slim figure seemed to glide across the wooden floor as he walked. The lines in his copper colored face were becoming more apparent as the years rolled by. He had a slight mustache that seemed to sprout in his teen years but then changed its mind about making a full appearance. His mind raced back and forth, but steadied a moment as he recalled the day before.

     Henry had told him that Linda was coming back to town. He didn't quite know what to say when he heard the news. After the ruckus they had caused before she headed off to Chicago, he was afraid to look happy about her returning to Macklin, or for that matter even disappointed. He just gave Henry an ordinary, "Is that right?" He really didn't expect too much of a reaction from Henry since Linda was one of his least favorite people. Still and all, Dyson remembered that last day she was in town two years before.

*        *        *

"Dyson I'm not sayin that I'm goin forever, I'm just sayin that I got to go for now."

"What you talkin bout gal? All I done for you and you just up and leave just like that?"

"Dyson I just need to get away from this place and these nosy folks. I can't stand people minding my business all the time. Ms. Erma and Ms. Odessa be practically camping out in front of this place at night. God knows they ain't got no business being down this way as much as they do."

"Since when you care bout what other folks think about you? I... I love you Linda. I ain't never loved a woman like I love you." His hands slid over her behind.

Linda knocked them away.

"Not even your wife?"

Dyson was silent for a moment.

"My wife? Linda, I told you..."

"Don't bother Dyson. It don't matter no way. Ok?"

"But I done told you over and over woman – she wasn't none o' my wife."

*        *        *

Dyson focused on the blue sky from his kitchen window. His body tingled with anticipation, even though he didn't know what to really expect. Linda had been living in a big city for two years. Maybe he wouldn't be good enough for her anymore. She was 20 years younger than he was but he never cared about that. He only cared about her full lips and her plump behind, hypnotizing him and bringing him into subjection. He admitted to himself a thousand times before, but one more time wouldn't hurt. He was still in love with Linda Hicks.

# 6

The house was awakened by Hester's cries. Annie slowly got out of bed, touching her leaking breasts, and Henry lay there quiet as always. Annie picked up Hester and heard a door in the house slam shut. She peaked out of the bedroom to see where Linda was headed this time of morning.

"I done seen you Annie, you might as well come on out of there." Linda strolled to the kitchen while looking toward the slit in Annie's door.

"This lil girl started hollerin like a banshee, so I was up anyway bout to feed her." Annie walked out of the bedroom.

"She sho is a sweet lil thing. Looks just like you spit her right out."

They sat down at the kitchen table.

"Well, I think she looks like Henry, she just..."

"Got your color huh?" Linda finished Annie's sentence. "Annie there ain't no sense in you dancin all around somethin like that."

"Chile you know I ain't never cared about that stuff. Mama was always the one talkin bout it all the time. I knew I was gone love my child no matter how bright or dark she came out. Just cause she bright don't make her no more special than nobody else in this world."

"Maybe not in the rest of this world, but it's gone make a hell of a lot of difference here in Macklin and you know it."

"I'm not gone start that with my children Linny. Henry and me done already talked about that."

"Well, Henry aint' no expert on the subject. Shoot, why you think he married…"

Linda stopped herself from saying it.

"I don't care what people said about the Moss boys. I know Henry loves me for *me*. He don't care one way or the other." Annie shifted Hester in her arms.

"I didn't mean it like that Annie. It's just that all those Moss boys married high yellow women, from his daddy on down. I ain't sayin Henry don't love you, but your being bright sho didn't hurt."

The room got quiet. Linda stood up to pour the coffee she'd put on.

Annie wanted to change the subject. She burped Hester, put her in her crib and walked over to the ice-box.

"I can put on some breakfast for you."

"Naw thank you. I'll be going out in a little while anyway. I know mama is probably dyin to see me." Linda laughed sarcastically.

"Well no matter what she said before you left Linny, I think she really do miss you." Annie turned and swayed a little, almost losing her balance.

"You alright?"

"Yeah, I'm alright. I gets like this in the morning nowadays."

"Why?"

"I'm having another baby, Linny."

"Oh," was all Linda could muster. She didn't know why.

"We're hopin for a boy this time. Henry wants a boy to name after him."

"Yall sho didn't waste no time did yall? I hope you don't plan on being like Viola Taylor. That woman'a put a rabbit to shame."

"Please! And anyway I *got* a husband. And we gone have as many as God'll give us."

Linda stood from the table taking her last sip from her cup.

"Well, I'm happy for you. Just one more pretty little baby for me to love."

"Thank you." Annie couldn't hide her smile. "Speaking of babies, when you plan on havin one of your own?"

"Annie Hicks!"

"It's Moss now Linny."

"Sorry… Annie Moss! Anyhow, you know mama would go crazy if I did… with no husband."

"Well, didn't you and Eddie try?"

"Honey the only thing Eddie was *tryin* to do was two-time his wife. This the very reason I'm right back here now." Linda became quiet again.

Annie was sorry she brought the subject of Eddie up again.

"Well, maybe you'll meet somebody soon, and who knows what'll happen."

"Yeah, who knows what'll happen." Linda's tone was flat. She took another deep breath and stood. "You sho you don't wanna stay for breakfast?"

"Naw, I better be getting on out of here. I'll be back later." Annie wasn't certain as to where Linda's first stop would be, but still she gave it one guess.

She walked to the front window and watched the back of Linda until she disappeared. She never understood what Linda ever saw in Dyson, but she thought about what Reverend Poe would say sometimes. *Money answereth all things.*

Henry walked into the kitchen and kissed Hester's forehead.

"How my beautiful girls doin this mornin?"

"Just fine."

"Uh-oh." Henry immediately sensed Annie's tone. "What I miss?"

Annie slowly poured the eggs on a plate. Her voice was monotone.

"Henry?"

"What is it baby?"

"If I was a… dark… woman, would you still wanted to marry me?"

Annie never looked up from her task.

"Oh Lord. What Linda done filled your head with now, Annie?"

"Linda?"

"Yeah Linda, your trouble-makin' sister. I don't know what she come her tail back here for. All she know how to do is stir up mess!"

"Henry I just asked a question, ain't no need for you to get your nostrils flaring."

"Well mighty funny you ain't never asked me such'a thang till now ain't it?" He snatched a bucket from the cupboard and headed outside to do his morning chores.

Annie slammed the spoon she had in her hand on the counter. Linda always had a way of putting thoughts into her head.

She listened to Henry take his anger out on everything he came in contact with. She convinced herself to still be happy that Linda was back. It was no surprise that Linda and Henry didn't see eye to eye. Linda never thought much of the Moss boys because she believed that they were all "color struck." Annie knew that Linda had a fling with Henry's brother David, and his wife, Roxy, had never let him live it down.

Annie and Henry were visiting David and Roxy one day and she had overheard them talking about Linda. Although Roxy's voice was an attempted whisper in the next room, Annie had heard every word.

"If I hear-tell of you ever talking to that spook Linda Hicks again, so help me I will kill you dead David." Roxy's words flew at him like an angled sword.

David had heard Dyson and a few other men bragging about Linda all over town and wanted to know what the fuss was about. She was different from Roxy. Her cocoa skin seemed to glisten in the sun even on a wintery day. She was beautiful but a little on the dark side from what he had been taught to consider pretty. Still, he couldn't resist the gentle tug that coaxed him almost daily. Then one August night, he too gave in to the temptation of Linda.

David had run into her a few times in town. On one occasion, she was wearing a tight, fiery red dress unlike one that he had ever seen. It had gold stars embroidered throughout.

The low-cut top revealed her ample breasts that seemed to be beckoning to him and he was ready to indulge. He smiled at her, and the rest would be a story told a hundred different ways.

# 7

Linda walked through the grass still damp with dew. She really missed the wetness against her ankles in the morning. Chicago never offered a summer morning like Macklin. She picked some wild flowers along her walk to Dyson's house. He only lived about two miles from Annie and Henry, so she knew that she would catch him still around the house. It was getting close to eight o'clock and the sun was making its grand appearance. On the way to Dyson's, she passed Ms. Erma's place. Just like always, she was sitting on the porch, pretending to be too busy to notice people passing. She was always either shelling peas or doing her knitting. Linda was too focused on her journey to care which this particular morning.

"Hah you doin this mownin?" Ms. Erma sang out, making sure Linda knew that *she* knew just where she was headed.

"I'm fine Ms. Erma. How bout ya self?"

"The Lawd still good to me like always. I don't make it round good as I used to, but I'm grateful for what he done thus far. Mm hmm." Ms. Erma was not more than 50 years old, but people would say that her hard life had aged her quickly. Her best friend, Ms. Odessa, was at least 20 years older, but the two of them were still as close as twins.

"Well that's good now Ms. Erma, I'll be seeing you hear?"

"Ok baby. You tell ya mama and nem I said hey."

"I will Ms. Erma."

As she continued walking she saw Ms. Odessa coming from beside the house. The two lived right beside each other. Linda was glad to be a little distance from them by this time. She had a clean escape and just waved to Ms. Odessa. Ms. Erma didn't waste any time before she shared her sharp intuition with her friend.

"I give you one guess where she headin this time o' mownin."

"Chile if you gat to guess, then something is sho nuff wrong with you." They cackled.

Ms. Erma shook her head while still shelling her peas.

"I tell you that gal well on huh way to givin Shirley Brown some flat out competition."

"Ooooh wee!" Odessa closed her eyes and shook her head. "Now that woman know she was a mess!"

"When dat woman left Macklin, erry man from here to Calhoun County went crazy!" Ms. Erma slapped her knee.

The women got such a kick out of themselves that they didn't notice Reverend Poe, the pastor of the church in Macklin, driving past.

"Mownin ladies."

"Mownin Reverend Poe." They both said in unison.

He stopped the car but didn't get out. He continued to talk from the window.

"Ah hope to see yall tomorrow at church. Ah'm sho lookin forward to yo caramel cake sister Erma."

"And I'll have your poke chops jest how you like em too reverend." Ms. Odessa added.

"Ah sho thank you both. Well, ah bettah be gettin' on. Gotta visit Sister Ruthann today." He drove along, moving at a pace where he might as well have been walking.

The two women started up again.

"That Reverend Poe is a good man, but ah sho feel sorry for him sometime." Ms. Erma tried her best to put on a sincere face. "Having to lead a bunch of folks like these here in Macklin sho couldn't be easy."

"Ain't dat the truth?" Odessa agreed. "Lawd knows half of em ain't nothin but some hypocrites, and the other half ain't livin a nickel's worth of dog meat." They laughed till they cried.

*    *    *

Linda neared Dyson's place and felt her stomach turning in knots. She told herself that she was being silly, that it was just the same old Dyson. But she still couldn't stop her palms from sweating or her head from spinning.

She came up to the door and just stood there. Before she could even knock, Dyson was there pulling the door open.

He, too, stood there for a moment like he was suspended in time, then he broke the silence.

"Linda. How…"

"You gonna just let me stand out here all day?" She invited herself inside without embracing him.

"I haven't seen you in two years gal. The least I can get is a hug." He stood there with his hands out.

"It's just me Dyson, and I'm not some long lost woman you barely know." She walked around the tiny front room. "What you got to eat in here?"

"Woman the only thing I want to taste right now is you."

"Now you talking like the Dyson I know."

She walked toward the bedroom after Dyson, wondering if her appearance was as cool as she hoped. She wanted things to remain the same between the two of them, so she had to wear the rough exterior at all times. She knew that she would have to let Dyson have his way with her one good time before she moved on to her next plan.

Dyson turned around toward her, his penis already thickening in his pants.

"You know, you still as pretty as a spring day. Ah didn't thank you could get any prettier than you was, but I been made a lie."

"Dyson, you think every woman in this town is pretty, so what that mean to me?" Linda loosened up, and became at ease. "Did you miss me?"

"Course I did woman. Ah ain't had a good night's rest since you left here. Ah didn't know what you was gonna face up there in Chicago."

"Well I'm back. So I hope you ain't got no other heffahs sniffin around here."

Dyson just watched her in amazement. He untied the straps on her dress and waited for her to undress him. He loved for her to take charge. He made up his mind right then to marry Linda and never let her out of his sight again.

# 8

The sun was high in the sky, and the humidity gripped the air making it impossible to feel the least bit of a breeze. A fly circled around Ruthann while she napped in the parlor. Earlene fanned herself with a piece of cardboard as she made her way to check on her grandmother.

She came close and leaned down to make sure Ruthann was still breathing. Ever since Ruthann had turned 90, Earlene became overly attentive and it bugged Ruthann to no end.

"Gal if you don't get somewhere and sat down you bettah!"

Earlene jumped and stepped back a few paces.

"Mama I'm just makin sho you alright. Don't you start gettin yourself upset over nothin now."

"Ah ain't gettin upset. Ah'm tired o' yall always fussin round here over me. Ah ain't feeble minded. The good Lawd ain't taken away mah sense."

Earlene knew what was coming next. Whenever the old woman got started, she would always talk about her days on the Windham Plantation. Earlene and her children had sat through countless lectures on Ruthann's days as a slave.

"Ah ran a whole plantation when ah wasn't but yea high. Ah..."

"I know mama." Earlene's tone was flat. "We really appreciate that, but right now you need to get ya rest." She didn't want to really get Ruthann going.

"I'm going out back mama. Call me if you need somethin."

"Ah ain't gonna need nothin but fuh yall to leave me alone. You heard what Reverend Poe say when he was here this mownin. The Lawd is taken good care o' me."

"Reverend Poe ain't no doctor mama. You get you some rest."

"Good. That's all ah want." Ruthann grunted, always having to have the last say.

Earlene headed back to her bedroom. Jeb had gone over to Pike's to pick up some wire to repair the chicken coop. She rambled through her drawer looking for something but forgot what it was. She wondered why Linda hadn't been by the house yet. Her train had come in the day before, but Earlene still hadn't laid eyes on her oldest daughter in two years.

She had been ambivalent about Linda leaving. She didn't want to let her go, but she decided it was just as well with the rumors that were floating around town about her. She was being compared to Shirley Brown, a woman who came to Macklin and upset every woman from there to Boon County. Earlene couldn't bear Linda having to deal with such a scandal.

Her feelings about Dyson were valid as far as she was concerned. He was too old for her daughter. He was not a handsome man, and he only had good use of only one of his hands. That was enough for Earlene to know that he didn't suit any daughter of hers.

As for her, no man could ever measure up to the high standards that she set in her mind for both Linda and Annie – especially Annie. Even though she felt deep in her heart that Henry was just as whorish as the two-timing stock he came from, she was satisfied knowing that he loved and took care of Annie. With Annie being the light-skinned one, Earlene just expected better of her.

Linda hadn't married by the time she turned eighteen. She was seeing quite a few men around town, but mostly Dyson by the time she left Macklin. Earlene had grown weary of hearing people whisper about Linda within her earshot. God only knew what they said behind her back. If they said half the things that they had said about Shirley Brown, then getting out of Macklin was the best thing for Linda.

Earlene remembered how the women in town had talked about Shirley Brown after Paul Jessup had died. Whether it was in Pike's, outside of church, or in somebody's kitchen, the women in Macklin never ceased from talking about it. She would listen as each woman gave her respective speech on the woman who turned Macklin upside down.

# 9

# Shirley Brown
## Macklin, Mississippi 1925

## Odessa Phillips

Reverend Poe got some nerve tryin to put that snake Paul Jessup in Glory, especially when he died huffin and puffin on top of that jezebel Shirley Brown. Lawd knows ah was jest doin my Christian duty when I helt Margaret's hand at that funeral. Not that she didn't know what Paul was up to, shucks the whole town knowed what he was up to. Good thang Shirley used the lil' sense God give her and stayed her home wrecking behind away from that funeral.

Out of all the counties in this here part of the world, she had to choose Caleb to do her business in. But I ain't gonna put *all* the blame on that gal, 'cause like my mama used to say, *You can't stop no bird from flyin over yo head, but you can sho stop him from makin a nest up there!* That Paul Jessup might as well been a hundred foot tall tree chile, 'cause he done made a nest with every loose goose that done flew his way!

And just to think Margaret cryin her eyes out and makin herself sick over that man, when he done left her to deal with the shame of his scandal. That Shirley Brown still walkin round here like she on top o' the world, when she ought to be too shame to leave her house. I declare –

the second that woman stepped her big toe into Macklin the men round here went crazy! Even the ones you would never believe in your life would chase up behind a woman like dat was gatherin round her porch.

I don't know what she got between them legs of hern, but what some-ever it is done stirred up a cloud round here so thick you bout need an ax to chop through it.

Poor Margaret. Ain't easy for a woman to accept somethin like this. I thank my maker every day that my Zeb was a decent Christian man – rest his soul. But iffin he was alive today and got caught up with the likes o' that Shirley Brown... I'd kill 'im!

# Erma Upshaw

Long as I been livin' I ain't never seent nobody as loose hip-ted as that gal Shirley Brown. Moved in here in serch a hurry you would think the law was after her for sho. Hmph, they tell me wasn't the law that was after her, but a woman that was good and ready to scratch her eyes out. You ask me there ain't but one thang make another woman mad enough to hurt her own kind – and dat's messin' with her man, chile!

Don't believe me, jest ask miss Lucy Craw. Honey she'll tell you all about it. Shirley tried once and only once to sliver up her Ron's pants leg, and Lucy was on her so quick! Ms. Shirley learned not to mess with Lucy's man and nobody else who even look like 'im. Anyhow, that heifer came here and stirred up so much mess round here it's a cryin shame. The bickerin that goes on round here don't make a bit o' sense, and it's always over somebody's man.

Ever heard of a woman who don't want no man of her own but will lie down and die jest to have yourn? Well, that's probably what they oughta put on that Shirley Brown's tombstone. God knows she done been through enough men round here to start a riot.

Not all the time was she out scroungin' the road for anythang in pants. She stayed in the house quite a bits. I used to talk to her from time to time, and she can hold a decent conversation too.

I tried to talk some sense in the gal 'cause it's just a shame for her to be the enemy o' the world. But honey, somebody make up they mind to do somethin, and ain't nothin you can do bout it.

I even told her bout how Jim Thomas tol' everybody that his daddy's hog pin smelled better than her naked behind, but it sho didn't stop her from rompin under the covers with him one bit!

Then I tried to tell her bout Sam Richards, that lowlife two-timin' dog. He said that being with Shirley Brown was like going to some kind of show; give her yo ticket, which was usually some cheap wine, and you can go in and out as many times as you want to! 'Course she didn't pay me no mind bout that either, cause I still seed ole Sam headin' her way with a bottle of moonshine in tow. Mmph, no need in askin me how I knowed. These eyes done seed a many thangs day and night. 'Course in that Shirley Brown's case – it was mostly night.

# Lucy Craw

My mama always told me *Don't ever trust a woman who walk like she doin' a dance.* Never really knew what she meant til that heffah Shirley Brown sashayed her wild butt into Macklin. Smilin' in my face like I was her new best friend. Soon as I turned my back, she was all over Ron like a cat on a fresh scratchin' post. Of course Ron was so far gone he didn't know if he was comin or goin.

Ron is known for being nice to any and everybody, so when Ms. Thang come waggin' her tail in his face, all he could do was smile that dumb smile like all men do when they tryin' to keep their manhood from risin.

Now me, hmph I knew what that harlot was up to the minute I saw Ron's nose open up so wide a tractor could go through it. I guess she thought she was gonna take my husband right out from under me, but honey, Lucy Craw wasn't raised by no fools. I knew just what to do.

First, I had to take care of home. I had to make Ron see that hussy's no-good intentions. Then, I told him that it ain't normal for a woman to come visit a friend who gat a husband dressed in somethin' so short you can see all her pastures, and hers sho wasn't green! I told him that he wasn't goin' over to her place to fix another lamp, chair, or anything else she done broke up rollin' around with some man. He understood alright – 'cause he remembered the last time a woman threatened to come between us.

I don't guess he wanted to *accidentally* run into another frying pan. So he stopped goin' over to Shirley's place. Matter a fact, he never even looked her way no more. As for her, I think she gat the point when I left that baby doll full of holes on her doorstep. After that Ron was the furthest thing from her mind, and she was as friendly as she could be with me.

You ask me?  Now that's what I know bout a woman who walk like she doin' a dance – and I still don't trust 'em.

# 10

The sun seared the gravel on the road. The heat
cooked the mud from the previous night's rain, almost turning it into a thick river of lava. Unlike Saturdays, Sunday
mornings in Macklin were noisy with people walking, talking, and going about. The few cars in town headed toward
the church, while others walked.

Annie felt sick again this particular morning, but
forced herself to get ready for church. Henry had started
coming with her on Sundays once they were married.

People filed into the small church greeting one another like they had not seen each other in years. The
church building was steeped in age. The bricks cried in
desperation against the heat.

Reverend Poe was at the podium with his eyes
closed as if he was enjoying the singing that had yet to
begin. The lines in his face were creased and running together like cracked cement. He wore his dark skin as a
badge of having worked in the fields from sun up to sun
down. His large frame engulfed the makeshift pulpit, con-
firming his reign over his flock.

Once they got to the church, everyone greeted Annie and doted on Hester. Earlene came up and took the
baby from Annie's hands.

"Where your sister?"

"She ain't here mama as you can see."

"I know that gal – I got eyes. Where she hidin' herself and ain't been in town all of two days?"

"Mama please!" Annie said the words without looking at her mother.

"Shhh." Henry pulled Annie closer to him.

The congregation started to belt out a hymn "Drive ole Satan Away." Hands clapped and feet stomped as the dust from the floorboards danced in rapid formation around them. The more they sang, the more powerful the spirit became. Everyone had joined in by this time singing:

*Drive him away Lord,*
*Drive ole Satan away*
*Drive him away Lord,*
*Drive ole Satan away.*
*We don't need him here,*
*Drive ole Satan away*
*We don't want him here,*
*Drive ole Satan away.*
*He's a hinder Lord,*
*Drive ole Satan away*
*He's a hinder Lord,*
*Drive ole Satan away.*

Ms. Erma and Ms. Odessa sat on the front row fanning – the backs of their heads looked like two giant wheels. Their wide brimmed hats blocked most of the view.

Reverend Poe stepped up as the song ended.

"Chirren – Gawd loves us today." His voice echoed through the sanctuary and swept over not only their ears, but their entire bodies.

"If it wasn't for Gawd's love, we couldn't make it."

"That's right Reverend!" A voice shouted from the dense crowd.

Jeb squirmed in his seat next to Earlene. He was never quite comfortable under Reverend Poe's sermons. They felt more like accusations directed at him, exposing his many wrong doings. He sat there remembering his drunken rages and Earlene swearing to God that she was done. Somehow she always found it in her heart to forgive him.

The love that Reverend Poe was preaching about – Jeb was sure Earlene had. He stroked her shoulder as he continued to listen.

The windows were open, but it still felt like the heat was closing in on Annie. Henry fanned her endlessly, but she still felt faint. She got up from her seat.

"Where you going?" Henry's head snapped up to meet Annie's face.

"I need some air."

With each step she took, her feet were like stone. She looked at Lucy Craw sitting in the back row, and she heard the faded voice of Reverend Poe. Bright colors hopped before her eyes, and her body was heavy as if she was being submersed in murky water. She hit the floor, and it sounded like a bag of barley flour. Lucy got up and ran over to her.

As Annie lay there unaware of herself, her consciousness began to drift. Through a blanket of fog she saw Linda with a tear-stained face walking backward. She saw Dyson McCloud standing there. Blood, crimson red, streamed from his eyes like tears. She heard a baby crying – discovering its lungs for the first time. All of the scenes swirled before her and became a blur. As quickly as the images came, they vanished.

When Annie came to, Lucy was tugging at the collar on her dress – Lucy's hand fluttered like a hummingbird's wings as she fanned Annie.

Henry moved Lucy out of the way and wiped Annie's face with his handkerchief. Earlene stood over them rocking Hester in her arms. The church service had come to a complete halt.

Yells of "Jesus" and "Oh my Lawds," rang out and bounced off the thin walls.

"Annie baby, can you hear me?" Henry spoke loud – still wiping at her face.

"If she ain't dead ah know she heard you. You bout to bust huh eardrums boy." Ruthann couldn't help but to take charge.

"Get her up from there." Earlene commanded.

Annie slowly lifted her head. She stood up and struggled for her balance.

"Yall don't mind this. She just expecting another lil one – that's all." Henry said the words with pride.

People gasped and smiles overtook their faces. Earlene and Jeb were taken back, but happy.

"Get her home this minute!" Ms. Odessa demanded. "She needs all her rest."

Earlene hurried over to her daughter.

"Baby, why didn't you tell me? I'm coming with you. Henry, take this baby."

"Mama I have done did this before. I'll be alright. You go on back and enjoy the service."

"You sho?"

"Yeah mama."

The congregation slowly reformed and Reverend Poe admonished them to thank God for the new life on the way.

Annie rested while Henry looked after Hester for the rest of the afternoon. Earlene brought over some ham and potato salad after church, and Jeb and Ruthann were with her as always. They all sat and talked as the sun drew down on the house. Its orange glow rested on the walls of the tiny living room. They heard a car pull up outside the house. The thump of the car door slamming sent Henry to the window, and before he could reach it, Linda walked through the door.

She stood there for a minute, then forced a trite smile.

"Hey yall!" Everyone's eyes on her made her uneasy.

"Hey yall?" Earlene mimicked. "Is that all you got to say to us after you flounce your tail back here after two years?"

Linda embraced Earlene. The hug was stiff and awkward. She then went to Jeb and Ruthann.

"I'm just in a hurry. Dyson is outdoors waiting for me."

"Dyson?" Earlene's tone spoke for itself even though she only said his name.

"Is that why you wasn't at church today? Linda, you picking up just where you left off. I…"

"Mama, I'm in a hurry." Linda interrupted and started to walk toward the bedroom.

The room stood still for a moment. Ruthann stood up.

"Gal, don't you walk away from your mama like you somebody – you ain't too grown for me to lay you out."

As always Jeb was silent. He never got involved with disciplining the girls, especially Linda. He had always seen the way that Earlene made a distinct difference between Linda and Annie. He usually had to step in and be Linda's advocate, so as far as chastising went, he had always told Earlene that it was to be her job. Naturally, Earlene spoke up.

"I can handle this mama." She motioned for Ruthann to take her seat. Earlene turned to her defiant daughter.

"Your sister havin' another baby, and you oughta be here helping out with her – not prancing around with the likes of Dyson."

Linda was trying to resist the urge to argue with Earlene.

"I ain't got time for this mama. I know he ain't never been good enough for you but it ain't your problem. Now, I need to get some things and be on my way. Dyson's waiting."

Silence stung the air again, and Linda's movements in the other room held everyone else suspended where they were. Hester's laughs seemed out of place as the tension formed like a thick fog in the house. Linda came out and headed out of the door as she tossed her voice in one direction.

"Henry, Dyson said tomorrow evening be a good time to start on the lil place across the way for me."

"Alright," was all Henry could say.

The door closed and trapped them on the other side of a storm called Linda.

*       *       *

Annie's belly stretched over the months, weighing her petite body down. Her globe-shaped stomach represented her bottled up emotions. Just like the baby – they were ready to burst any day. Henry was spending most of his evenings fixing up the little shotgun house across the yard with Dyson. Linda had settled in it, but still helped Annie with Hester and the house chores.

Linda went to the fields for a while until Dyson told her she didn't have to anymore. He wanted to take care of her and said that he would work twice as hard as he usually did in order to do it. There had still been no wedding – Linda kept telling Dyson, "I didn't come back here to stay, man. Soon as I get on my feet I'm going to New York." This was enough to keep him at bay, but at times Linda didn't really believe it herself.

Fall had put up a fight to step aside, so that winter had come in mildly. This particular morning Annie looked outside. Frost had covered the porch like a sheet of light feathers. January brought with it a melancholy mood for her. She was ready to have the baby. Her appetite had left her and she slept often. Earlier that morning Henry rubbed her back and slowly kissed her neck. She moved his hand away –she hadn't felt like giving him any loving in months. Hester had been with Earlene for a few days to give Annie some rest.

Lucy Craw was coming over to make sure Annie got the help she needed. Lucy and Ron Craw had been in Macklin since Annie was a little girl. When they arrived, the legendary Shirley Brown was still wreaking havoc on the town.

Lucy walked up to Annie's porch. Her amber skin glowed in the winter sun. Her tiny freckles seemed to dance on her nose and forehead. She knocked on the door, then walked right inside.

"Annie, you in here?"

"Yeah, I'm here." Annie called from the kitchen. "Come on in. I put some coffee on."

"That's what I'm here for chile. You just sit on down and rest. God knows you ready to pop any second now." Lucy chuckled and pulled a chair from the table.

"Yeah, I feel so…"

"Heavy?" Lucy interrupted. "And you don't look so good neither."

They sat down at the table. Whenever Lucy talked, her hands led the conversation.

"It's probably a boy you got in there this time – they put you through hell before they get here, and then carry other women through it after they come."

Even through the laughter Lucy sensed that Annie wasn't her usual bubbly self.

"What's wrong with you girl? You lookin like Margaret Jessup round here."

"I guess that's how I feel Lu." Annie ran her hand through her curly mane.

"Now look, you ain't buried your husband, and then had to face folks *and* their two faces bout the *way* he died. Margaret Jessup had a reason to look like she did chile."

"I know I ain't buried my husband, but I sho feel like I done lost him." Annie sipped her coffee.

"Girl, don't you worry bout Henry. Shoot, he just a man. Soon as you have that baby he gone come around. You just wait." Lucy was sure of her words.

Even when she was trying to comfort someone else, Lucy had a way of telling her story just to encourage the other person.

"When I was pregnant with lil Ronnie I felt the same way. He was my second baby, and my last baby – thank God. Never did have the lil girl I wanted, but I guess that's why the Lord sent you my way."

"What make you so sure it's gone be a boy?" Annie asked, although she knew how people would always predict the sex of a baby by how low or high a woman was carrying.

"The way you carrying? "Humph, that's a baby boy if I ever seen one." Lucy confirmed Annie's suspicions.

"Now you sound like my grandma. She done decided that this was a boy a long time ago."

"See?" Lucy gestured with a wave of her milky hand. "I know Ms. Ruthann know what she talking about. She done caught enough baby tails in her hand *to know*."

Lucy stood up and walked to the icebox. "I swear that woman's got a set of eyes nobody can see."

Annie chuckled, "It ain't her eyes according to her. She always say,
*Heaven knows and tells me all its secrets.*

Lucy poured some milk in her coffee.

"I wish she can tell me if Ron is keeping his thang where it belongs!"

The two laughed hysterically.

"Chile why you always going on about that man putting that *thang* somewhere it don't belong?"

"Cause if a dog will stray away once, ain't nothin stoppin' him from doing it again – cept maybe my fryin' pan." Lucy smiled coyly and sipped at her coffee with her eyes closed.

Annie stood again – restless.

"I need to get dinner started." Annie wobbled back to the table with a bowl of snap beans.

"Oooh wee." Lucy shook her head. "Girl I sho wouldn't wanna be you right about now. I'm so glad my child rearing days is over I can dance a jig." Lucy wiggled her behind in the chair.

"Thought you said it was a beautiful thing?"

"Mmm hmm – it's real beautiful to look at, but ain't nothin pretty bout totin around a sack o' bricks on your belly for nine months."

"Lu what I'm gone do with you? You too much."

"I know." Lucy batted her lashes playfully. "Speaking of too much, how's that sister of yours doing?"

"She doin fine I guess. Henry and Dyson fixed up that lil house across the yard for her to stay in. It's coming along."

"Dyson huh?" Lucy crossed her legs and sucked her teeth. Annie searched her eyes and tried her best to read her inaudible thoughts.

"What you done heard now Lu?"

"Who me?" Lucy said, putting her hand on her ample bosom.

"Yes you. I know you get around, I know these folks in Macklin, and I know you may as well tell me what you done heard." Annie pointed her finger toward Lucy.

"Aw girl nothin I ain't heard around here already. I was in Pike's yesterday and Ms. Odessa was going on about Linda and Dyson to Reverend Poe's wife, as if that woman could care less. She too busy tryin to keep the good Reverend's eye from wandering."

"Aw Lu, let you tell it every man on God's earth go chasing behind other women."

"My mama always said, *Only thang you can put past a man is air.* And baby I believe her. You can't put nothin' past no man."

"I guess only Heaven knows if you right." Annie peered out of the kitchen window. The sound of the snap beans crackled as if they were conversation enough for the two of them.

# 11

Annie turned in her bed unable to rest. She dreamt that she was tussling with a man twice her size. His fists pounded on her stomach and she couldn't escape his grip. She fought like fire, but to no avail. Just when she decided to give up and surrender to her opponent, the light seeped into the corner of her eye. The brightness suddenly revealed that the man wasn't really there, but her pain was all too real.

The baby was making its way – announcing its anticipation. She felt the slickness between her thighs and called out for Henry. He was walking from the outhouse and heard her cries. He ran as best he could through his sluggishness. He quickly got through the yard and to the bedroom. He found her curled up in the bed, moaning like a lamb.

"Get my grandma." Annie managed to get the words out.

"I'll go get Lucy and have her stay with you til I get back." Henry was breathless, but managed to get his coat on and frantically maneuvered across the bedroom.

Annie wanted Linda there, but she knew that Linda was at Dyson's place. She was sure that Linda would be there for the birth of her second child, especially since she was in Chicago when Hester was born. Annie gathered the sheets under her bottom, trying to make herself halfway comfortable.

The brightly lit morning fooled her senses. The air was chilly, but the sun was high in the sky. She wanted

Henry to hurry. She heard the front door burst open, and soon after, Lucy came ripping through the house. Seemingly all in one moment of time, before Annie knew it, Lucy was at her side.

"I'm here girl, b*ut where the hell is Linda?*" Lucy mumbled the last part under her breath.

Lucy ran and grabbed fresh sheets and towels from a chest in the kitchen. She went into the room and Annie was hanging halfway out of the bed.

"You sho got quite a start to your day huh?" Lucy laughed trying to lighten the mood. She kept talking as she hurried around the room.

"Shoot, Adam and Eve did a number on us. When God said man had pissed Him off he wasn't lying. He said the man had to toil on the land and the woman had to go through this mess?" Lucy sighed and rolled her eyes. "I think I'd rather been chopping all the cotton in Mississippi if Ron could have gone through this here!"

No matter what the circumstances, Lucy was known for her candor.

"It ain't all that bad Lu." Annie took short breaths. "Women been doin this since the beginning of time. Besides, like you said, my grandma done caught more babies than you can bat your eyes at."

"Yeah, her stories of them old plantation days still make me thank my maker that I ain't never had to be no slave." Lucy held Annie's hand.

Lucy and Annie heard Henry drive up. Earlene helped Ruthann out of the car and like they had done before, they left Hester with Jeb. As they walked in the house, Henry knew that he was to be as far away from the room as possible. When Hester was born, the women had ordered him to stay out until after Hester was screaming for dear life, which was his cue to enter the room.

Ruthann's very presence commanded reverence among the women in the room. Her years had not kept her from her calling as a midwife. Her hands were thick with veins that bulged as emblems of honor. Although her arthritis had flared over the years, she insisted on delivering her grandchildren, her great-grand children, and now her second great-great grandchild.

She ordered Earlene and Lucy about.

"Lucy, boil me some water, and get her out that bed so we can put some clean sheets on it. Earlene, get me the ironing board to put under this mattress."

The women slowly pulled Annie to her feet, and Earlene held her up by her shoulders as she caressed her head. Earlene had remembered when Ruthann delivered Annie and Linda. She couldn't believe how fast the years had gone by.

Earlene's own mother had died of pneumonia when she was six, and Ruthann raised her and her four younger siblings. Earlene was the oldest and along with Ruthann and John, her grandfather, she became a surrogate mother to them all. She swore to herself that when she did have children of her own, she didn't want a brood. She would be modest in her child-bearing. It took her years to forgive her mother for dying and leaving five children behind.

Her father had skipped town and ended up married to another woman and had eight more children. Earlene was even more hurt because Ruthann never had a kind word to say about her father. Ruthann never even called his name, which was Isaiah. She always referred to him as "the no-good scoundrel." She would often go on a tirade when the children started getting out of hand, and always within earshot of Earlene. *What kinda man up and leave his chirren when his wife ain't cold good yet? No good scoundrel didn't even have the gumption to say goodbye. Heaven knows that man gonna get his.*

Ruthann's words resonated through Earlene's bones. Even as Annie lay there travailing, Earlene thought of her own life and those tough years of her own marriage. With each scream that bolted from Annie's lungs, Earlene held her tighter – attempting to suffocate the memories, but they continued to persevere.

All the gray memories rested on Earlene like a shadow through the birth of her second grandchild. The days when Jeb chose the grain alcohol over her embrace pushed through her – just like the baby was pushing through Annie's womb.

Another scream from Annie, and Earlene remembered the last time Jeb had come home drunk.

*     *     *

Linda and Annie were young, around 7 and 9, and one of them had just gotten over a fever – she couldn't remember which one just now. She had finished dinner and the girls were helping with the dishes. Earlene could hear Jeb's car in the distance and the rushing sound of the engine as he stomped on the gas, then the hollow sound of him easing off. It would sound like a locomotive – drowning out the katydids and whippoorwills that led the night creatures in a harmonic band.

Whenever Jeb would come home drunk, Earlene would always have words for him. Linda and Annie would beg their mother not to say anything. They knew that this would only create a riot that would go on for hours, usually conceived out of Earlene's smallest comment. If he stumbled, Earlene would suck her teeth and say, "Just look at you. You can't even stand up good," and the war would be on.

Earlene would always agree to keep her lips and not say a mumbling word, but once Jeb stepped through the door, she could never hold her peace.

The car had finally reached the yard and came to a screeching halt. It sounded as if Jeb had sat in the car frozen. They heard nothing for a minute or so. The silence in the house was deafening and Earlene's face stoic. Minutes later they heard Jeb walk onto the porch and stumble over one of the chairs.

Earlene sent the girls to their room. She stood there in the living room, and then walked slowly toward the front door. She never said a word. She heard clamoring like steel against itself and Jeb cursing the air. She knew he had knocked over the chairs on the porch. Then after hearing a loud thump – she heard nothing.

She ran to the window in time to see that Jeb had passed out on the porch. It was late March she remembered, and there was still a nip in the night air. The faithful wife in her wanted to run to her husband's aid and help him into the warm house. She wanted to get some hot coffee in him and restore him back to himself, because whenever he drank, Earlene would always ask herself who this man was. It never seemed like Jeb.

Annie and Linda had come out of their room. They slowly walked into the front room. They saw Earlene standing there stark still. Then Annie looked up and asked, "You need us to help you bring daddy in again?" She shooed the child away with a wave of her hand. After being in deep thought, Earlene had quietly said, "No. Not this time baby."

Linda protested in her father's defense. "We can't just leave him out there mama. Let's go get him."

"I said no!" Earlene's voice was unyielding and firm.

Her other self had finally taken a stand. There was the sweet and humble wife who jumped at the sound of Jeb's every beck and call. But then there was the fed up woman who was tired of being tired of this horror that had taken over her marriage.

This was the side that would win the battle that night. She turned away from the window and said to no one in particular, "We gone leave him be."

The girls had climbed into bed with her that night. The still silence had rocked Earlene and Annie to sleep. Unbeknownst to Earlene, Linda had lain awake most of the night.

That next morning they were startled by a faint but consistent tapping on the door. Earlene rose to her feet and Linda was on her heels. She opened the door and Jeb stepped in – a film of frost had settled on his face. His body convulsed with shivers. He had wet his pants and the wetness had frozen and stuck to his pants like a layer of sugar. She still smelled the stench of grain alcohol on him – wafting from his pores.

At that moment, she thought how Ruthann would say that *Heaven knows and is watching all the time*. That morning, no words were exchanged. No battle was fought. No points were argued. Silence had crept in and stolen the show.

Jeb slowly walked through the house into the kitchen. Earlene followed him there and began making a fire in the stove.

Earlene had never forgotten that night. She had never forgotten the dawn's silence. That morning brought with it a resolution for which she had fervently prayed and would forever be grateful. Jeb never took another drink again.

*     *     *

Annie's screams ripped through the room. Earlene rubbed her arms and kissed her damp forehead. Lucy stroked her hair and reassured her from time to time with, "You doin just fine now."

Ruthann's hands moved like fine-tuned instruments. She was the calmest one in the room.

"Earlene bring me that sheet." She ordered from under Annie's outstretched legs. "This boy's in a hurry to get here."

Annie's breathing was labored. "How… how you know it's a boy grandma?"

"Cause Heaven knows and tells me all its secrets." Ruthann commanded her great-granddaughter's obedience. "Now hush up and push gal. Push!"

Annie squeezed with all her might – the force of the head crowning her womb felt like she was being ripped in two, yet she continued to push on Ruthann's command. Earlene and Lucy coached in unison, as if they were coaxing the baby out. One last push and the baby fell into Ruthann's hands. She quickly turned the baby around as Earlene folded the sheet around its tiny body. Ruthann cut the umbilical cord. Lucy had tears in her eyes. Annie fell back in exhaustion, but still managed a mumble.

"Let me see it… let me see my baby. What is it?"

As if everyone was ignoring her, Annie's patience grew thin. She raised her voice.

"Mama, I wanna see it. What is it?"

Earlene brought the baby up to Annie's chest. The smell of raw blood and sweat sifted up around them. She was moved by the thing that she still considered a miracle from God. She cuffed the baby onto her daughter's chest.

"It's a boy." Earlene's voice was composed. "You done had a little boy, baby."

Annie held him in her arms. She contemplated names in her head while the women cooed over him.

"You gonna name him for Henry?" Ruthann's voice was rough. "This is his first son. A man always want his first boy named for him."

"No ma'am." Annie smiled and kissed the baby. "His name gone mean something grandmamma. I just can't think of it just now."

"Lucy, go and get Henry and tell him he got a boy." Earlene touched Lucy excitedly, remembering that Henry was in the next room.

They cleaned the baby up and Henry came in. He went over to Annie and the baby and kneeled by the bed.

"Annie, that's our boy." Henry rubbed his tiny head. "What kind of name should we give him?"

"Look at him, Henry. He just telling us what his name should be with them eyes open just as wide as day. Look like he can see way down the line of times. I wanna name him Isaiah, just like the prophet."

"That be a fine name for a fine boy." Henry laughed.

Ruthann perched her lips, as she didn't want to interrupt the moment. She just kept thinking that she would now be forced to say a name that reminded her of a man whom she once believed wasn't fit to walk the earth. She supposed that the years had eased her contempt for her ex son-in-law. Looking at her great-great grandbaby, she was hoping that his face would bring some good to the name.

# 12

The seasons folded in and out, and the years announced themselves with urgency. Flowers blossomed and withered under charcoal skies. Life was given and taken away like a vapor. Vows were broken and bonds were sealed. Things changed and yet stayed the same.

Linda found herself still in Macklin, Mississippi after over four years had passed since she had first come back. Annie had a third child – another little girl. Linda and Dyson were still tending to each other's needs but had never married.

Last winter, Linda surprised everybody when she'd announced that she was having a baby. Annie was excited for her. Earlene and Jeb were too, but battled with their happiness because Dyson still hadn't married their daughter. Ruthann of course had her opinion on the matter. She mouthed on about not understanding why Linda and Dyson couldn't just get married and call it done. "That gal just got to do everything just like she wanna do it."

With their babies the same age, Linda and Annie spent more time together. All of Annie's children were the color of butter. Linda's child took after her with skin like deep fudge. Linda couldn't help but think about the future of her daughter in a place like Macklin. The town seemed to be steeped in unforgiving qualities when it came to children being born out of wedlock, and the lighter people still had disdain for people of a darker hue.

Certain people in town had always been accepted regardless of their dark skin. The Moss men were perfect examples. Some people said that it didn't matter because their family was well off and they would marry light women anyhow. At times Annie thought that Linda was out of her mind about the way she focused on color. She wished Linda could focus on something else for a change, especially since little Emma was here. When people saw Annie's children and Linda's daughter Emma in town, they would say how much they looked alike – except their coloring of course.

Linda didn't like it, but she understood the ways of the south. She remembered the stories that Ruthanne told them of her days as a slave.

*Color ruled everythang.* Ruthann would say. *Sometimes ah wished to God ah was born darker, jest so ah wouldn't have to be in that house with that snake Mr. Giddens. That man had an appetite for young slave womens that was unnatural and unholy. Ah would try my best to stay out his way, but being in that house tending to Misses it wasn't nothin' ah could do. One day ah was washin' clothes in the back of the house, and it was real hot. Ah kept on doin' my work, but ah saw ole Massa Giddens comin' up to me out the corner of my eye. My first instinct was to jest tear out and run. But ah knowed that if ah ran, ah would jest get it worse if he caught me.*

*He called me in the house – said he needed me to get somethin' nuther from the kitchen. Ah walked in the house behind him, scared out my mind. By the time we got to the kitchen, he came up to me and kissed me on the side of my face. Then he licked my face, and ah stepped back and looked straight at him, shakin' my head no. He slapped me and told me not to ever look him in the eye, or he would skin me alive. He dragged me to the pantry and pulled at my clothes.*

*What he did to me that day was the worse thang ah had ever knowed. Ah wasn't but bout fourteen years old then, and it didn't stop after that. It didn't stop either after ah had your grandmamma. Ah would pray that ah would be sent to the fields, but God answered another prayer instead. Ole Massa Giddens up and died in his sleep one night. Some folks say it was his heart. Humph, but ah knowed better.*

Even after all the stories, Linda hoped in her heart that Emma would grow up and marry a lemon-colored man. Dyson took to Emma from the day she was born. She didn't look like him because she was the image of Linda. Still and all, it bothered him when people would remind him of it.

On certain matters, Macklin would never change. When a baby was born, people talked. When somebody died, people talked. When somebody got married, they talked. When somebody got divorced, or cheated on – they talked. Earlene would often say, "These folks will gossip about the devil being a liar – and the preacher's house being on fire!"

Annie and Linda took the children to see Earlene one Saturday afternoon. The sun was beaming down on the house with a vengeance. The children were playing in the yard and the women sat under the pecan tree watching them. Earlene had made lemonade, and the ice had melted as soon as it hit the glass pitcher. Hester and Isaiah ran and jumped through the grass, while the babies Sarah and Emma, laughed and tried to keep up.

Earlene's words had already hit the universe before she could think about what she was saying.

"Annie you shouldn't let them chirren play in the sun too long – they'll get dar…"

At first Linda decided to pretend that she didn't hear her mother's remark. But since she now had a child of her own, she refused to let it go.

"Or what, mama? They'll get too dark?" Linda sat up in her chair. "Never mind about Emma huh? Just Annie's kids right? Oh – Emma is already black as midnight, so don't mind about her."

Earlene was immediately on the defensive.

"I didn't mean it that way chile."

"Then what did you mean mama? You know that's why I left this place six years ago. I swore I would never be back here. I'm not gone let you curse my child like you cursed me." Tears glistened on Linda's cheeks.

"Cuss you?" Earlene twisted her face in confusion.

Linda struggled with her words.

"Mama I remember when me and Annie was little and you took us to Jackson to visit your sister. Your family had never seen Annie and me, and you introduced us to them. You pulled Annie in front of you and doted on her. You said how she could sing and was smart in school and that she was gone be something special one day. When you got to me, all you said was, *This here is Linda, my other girl.*

Linda was standing, shifting the weight from each foot.

"Do you have any idea how much that hurt me mama?"

"Gal, I don't even remember what you talkin' bout."

"And that's the problem, mama. You…"

"That's enough!" Annie interrupted. "Do yall know how tired I get of hearing yall go on and on about color?"

Annie stood and put her arm around her sister.

"Linda, it don't matter – Emma is pretty just like you." She swung around in Earlene's direction. "And mama don't go making no difference between these  kids. It's just foolish."

The children's laughter echoed against the trees as the three women became quiet.  The leaves rustled, celebrating the light breeze that blew over the yard.  Earlene, Annie, and Linda cleared their minds of the conversation that had just happened.  They all knew, however, that the subject was anything but over.

## 13

Annie and Linda walked home practically in silence. Annie always tried to lighten the mood whenever Linda was upset.

"Linny, remember when we used to run up and down this road with no shoes on?"

Linda cracked a slight smile. "Yeah, I remember. Our lil feet would burn so bad it felt like they was gone catch fire."

"That's what I like to do Linny- I like to remember the good times we had."

They walked on and finally reached the farm. Linda headed across the field with Emma sleeping in her arms. Annie led the children into the house. Just as she reached the door, she looked out and saw Henry walking from behind the little house where Linda lived. She didn't give it a second thought. As she got the children settled, Henry came into the house.

"How's my sweetheart doin' this evening?" He kissed Annie on the back of her neck. "You have a nice visit at your mama's?"

Annie rubbed her eyes. "Yeah, we had a nice visit. I just wish things could be different between Linny and mama."

"Now you know your mama ain't gonna change for no – body." Henry sang the word no.

"I know Henry, but I know Linny got to feel bad cause mama did... sort of treat me a little better than her. Not just since we been grown either honey, all our lives." That was the first time Annie had ever admitted out loud the reality of the whole thing.

Henry slid his shirt over his head.

"Well Linda is just fine. You know don't nothing really get to her. Shoot – she made of steel."

"You don't know her like I do Henry. She's my sister." Annie paused, her mind suddenly going back to the moment she got home.

"What were you doing over there by the lil house?"

"I thought I saw a raccoon out there, but it wasn't nothing. He changed the subject. "How soon dinner be ready?"

"In a lil while." Annie looked at Henry. "Honey, you ever talk to Dyson about Linda?"

Henry didn't like to discuss people – he always felt that to speak "of" someone was the same as gossiping. His mother had once given him a lesson on the subject. One of his friends tried to turn him against another friend. His mother was very careful about training her boys. She had said plainly one day, "When somebody talks to you about somebody else, then sure as shootin' they gone talk to somebody else bout you." She summed it up by simply saying, "If a dog will bring a bone, he'll carry a bone."

Henry was reluctant.

"What would I have to say about Linda to Dyson?"

"I mean," Annie said with her hand on her hip, "Does Dyson ever talk about Linda? About marrying her?"

"I don't know Annie. The two of them talk about it sometime I guess. But Linda still married to that musician fella – what his name?"

"Eddie?" Annie turned her face up. "That marriage wasn't no good cause he was still married to that Vickie whoever." Annie was whipping cornmeal in a bowl like it was being punished.

"Well he still writes Linda every now and again." Henry said nonchalantly. Then his tone suddenly changed. "Gal I don't know bout they business."

Annie was adamant.

"Seems strange to me that Linda and Dyson done had a child together, and took 'em three years mind you – and they still ain't married yet."

"Maybe she don't want to marry him Annie. Is you thought about that?"

"I don't know what I thought. It's just that Emma don't look a thing like Dyson. Seem like that child ought to been kind of brown – with Dyson being yellow. But Emma just as dark as…"

"Linda." Henry interrupted. "Baby, how can you talk about color when you know how it's done hurt Linda so?"

Annie stopped whipping the cornmeal.

"I'm not saying there's something wrong with being dark. I married you didn't I?"

"Yeah, you married me." Henry looked at Annie. "Maybe to spite your mama."

Henry knew he had struck a nerve. He couldn't believe that he had said it, but it was too late. Annie didn't have to say a word. The look in her eyes had said enough. Her voice was laced with let-down.

"I married you because I love you." Annie was sincere.

"I know baby." Henry hugged Annie tight. "But I done heard what your mama say bout us Moss boys one too many times. *Them boys jest as black as night, but they always gat to have a high yellow gal to give them some babies.* Henry mimicked Earlene, twirling his neck and rolling his eyes for effect. "This town ain't been so kind to me neither baby. I done had my share of hurt too being dark as I am." Henry stepped back from Annie.

"You?" Annie stepped back. "Henry these people in Macklin been kissin' up behind your family for as long as I can remember."

"Is that right?" Henry looked blankly at Annie. "When me and Dyson go into town – seem like white folks know he's a nigger too, but they seem to treat him a little better. A nigger is a nigger to them, but a dark nigger is something else altogether."

In all the years they had been married, Annie had never heard Henry speak about those things. She stood there and wondered how the "color-stricken" demon had come into her home. Then she remembered that she was the one who brought the subject up in the first place. Her world had stopped for a moment, and she realized that there was no escaping this thing. It was bigger than her, bigger than her marriage, and bigger than the small town of Macklin.

Annie's attempt to innocently chat with her husband had gone awry, yet she still pondered on why Emma was so much darker than Dyson. Then she thought about her children being light even though Henry was dark.

The thought left her mind because it started to give her a headache anyway.

\*     \*     \*

Dyson had been waiting for Linda when she came home. He missed her whenever she was gone for the shortest bit of time. When he wasn't working, his goal was to be at Linda's dress tail. Linda resented his clinginess, but at the same time, she loved the attention.

He kissed her slowly and nudged his hardness against her behind. She did enjoy sex with Dyson – more so the act than the partner. She fully participated in every move and motion, but her mind was usually someplace else. She still fantasized about Eddie at times. At other times, she thought about being with the other man that she had kept to herself.

Dyson groaned and collapsed on top of her. She slid from under him and made her way to the dresser. Dyson always tried to reach out to her.

"What's wrong baby?"

Linda pulled her belt to her robe tight around her waist.

"Nothing."

"Linda, you want to get married? Is that it?"

"What make you think I wanna get married Dyson?"

Dyson stood up. He still wanted more of Linda.

"We got a child, and people talking, and ..."

"You think I care about what these folks in Macklin think? Shoot, let 'em talk. They ain't got to raise nor feed this child."

Linda endured the whispers and the funny looks. She even bore the outright harassing when she was pregnant with Emma. It wasn't her plan to get pregnant before marriage. She hadn't gotten pregnant in over three years, and she and Dyson didn't take precaution. She still thanked God for Emma despite how she had come to be. In Linda's eyes, God wasn't capable of making any mistakes.

# 14

The war came and Macklin felt the brunt of it in more ways than one. Mothers mourned their sons, and wives mourned their husbands. Dyson would have gone, but his handicap hindered him. Henry had not gone away either, and Annie was grateful.

It seemed that everything was rationed. Stamps were needed to buy the children's shoes, sugar, and even gas. Annie couldn't help but to feel like the war was zapping the strength from everybody in Macklin. With the war came the news of Linda expecting another child. Earlene was furious but felt it was out of her control.

Viola Taylor had another baby – her tenth. Nobody even bothered to care anymore one way or the other how the children came to be. Her babies just seemed to appear out of thin air. She had invited some people over after church one Sunday. Ms. Erma and Ms. Odessa had graced the little house with their presence as always after the birth of one of Viola's children. Lucy Craw never missed a chance for the latest gossip. Earlene, Ruthann, and Annie had brought most of the food for dinner.

The women knew how to lend a helping hand to each other when it was needed. Even though Viola had a house full of children, it always managed to be quiet whenever she had company. This time the stillness came because Viola had sent the other children out to play after they had eaten.

She couldn't wait to spin her latest tale about the newest baby's no count father. The rumor in town was that it was Hank Simmons' child, who was married of course to the waitress who worked at Blake's tavern; Viola had a different story. She said that this child's father wasn't Hank's, but the man did have a family. Everybody knew that she didn't care one way or another about having babies, despite the fact that they belonged to somebody who wasn't available. As far as Viola was concerned, a baby was a blessing no matter how it got here. She always said that she would have as many children as the good Lord blessed her with. Lucy Craw would always tease her and say, "Well the good Lord need to bless somebody else!" Even though the little kitchen was full of talk about babies, fathers, and husbands, the war still inched its way into the conversation.

"I tell you this war ain't doing nobody a bit o' good." Ms. Erma shook her head in disgust. "I can't believe how they gat these boys dying in a war that they ain't gat no business fightin' in the first place."

"Say that again." Ruthann nodded in Ms. Erma's direction. These wars kill the wrong peoples. Ah was bout 18 when the Civil War come, and ah remembers it well."

The talk had gone on for hours, when Viola wanted to know where Linda was hiding herself. Although she had no room to talk about anybody, Viola reveled in the fact that Linda was unwed and pregnant too. She felt that it was justice in a way, especially since Earlene looked down her nose at women like her. When Viola was pregnant with her fifth child, she remembered how Earlene cut her eyes at her in church. Reverend Poe was preaching about the virtuous woman in the book of Proverbs. Earlene had looked at Viola and turned the corners of her mouth up. Viola practically read her thoughts and knew that Earlene was just boiling over with a, *You need to keep them legs closed for once.*

So quite naturally Viola made it her business to ask about Linda. This way, she knew that when the women left and talked about her behind her back – they would have somebody else to talk about too.

"So where miss Linda keepin' herself now days? Is she doing alright with this baby?"

Earlene could tell by the excitement in Viola's question that it wasn't out of genuine concern.

"She doing fine. She didn't feel up to coming out this evening, but she doing fine."

Viola pushed on. "So you say she how far long now?"

"I didn't say." Earlene spat.

"Well I'm just asking Ms. Earlene."

"I be fine if you don't just *ask*. Why don't you worry bout these lil heathens of yours runnin' round here without a daddy to first."

"Now Ms. Earlene, I can't sit here and let you insult me in my own house."

"Then I'll just leave your house."

Annie stood up.

"Wait just a minute. There ain't no cause for all this. We just talkin' and having a good time. Viola you done had a baby not hardly two days ago, so don't get yourself all upset. And mama, it ain't right for you to talk that way to Viola in her house. Now you need to tell her you sorry."

The room got quiet. Annie's words were supposed to bring peace. Instead, they practically invited the tension into the hot July air. Water ran down the pitcher of tea sitting on the table. Ruthann started to hum an old hymn.

Ms. Erma and Ms. Odessa sipped their tea, waiting for the next word. Lucy finally broke the silence.

"Look here, there's already a stupid war going on across the sea. We don't need one up in here either. Now I don't know bout yall, but I'm waitin' to taste some of that pecan pie Annie brought in here."

The tension slowly lifted from the kitchen, and the normal gossip picked up where it left off. They talked about Helen Lane and how she was on her third husband. They talked about Richard Jenkins and how he left his wife with nine children. Macklin was small, but the population was bursting with children. It seemed as if a baby was born every other month in town. They talked about Cindy Lee, and Joyce Riggins – how both of their babies had died after they did laundry during the holidays. Anybody ought to have known that it was bad luck to wash between Christmas and New Years day. Washing on a Sunday *and* between Christmas and New Years was like giving evil the keys to your house and rolling out the welcome mat.

Coincidence had no place in Macklin. Everything operated on cause and effect. No one ever went fishing on a Sunday because you would catch the devil. Old man Gene Tillman was blind in one eye because he stared at the stars too long one night, and Ms. Erma had sworn that she witnessed the very act. When her husband died, she refused to stay in the house where they had lived for twenty some odd years. She swore that his spirit would lurk about the place. It happened to Ms. Odessa, so it would certainly happen to her. Their children thought the two women were crazy. But they never failed talking about "haunts" and what not. As they talked about those things, Ms. Erma thought about her own life.

Ms. Erma had four children by the time she was twenty. She married when she was a girl of fifteen. She married partly because she felt it was the thing to do – and partly because her uncle wouldn't leave her alone. Her first baby was a little boy that she named James, after his father. She had three girls right after him, and she named them Cassie, Bessie, and Flossie. When they were little girls, their friends would sing their names like it was a song. "Big" James was a preacher's son from Wayne County.

Ms. Erma was the oldest of six children and was always playing mother to some screaming baby. James said that he would give her anything she wanted, within his means of course, if she would just marry him. So at 15, she went from her parents' house to her husband's house. She didn't mind cooking and cleaning up for James because she had been doing that for her whole family since she was ten. What she did mind were his fists on her every other night.

Ms. Erma never spoke a word of the beatings, even after James had died. She had never even told Ms. Odessa, her closest friend and confidant. The women made each other believe that they knew everything about the other, but the truth was, they only revealed the parts of their lives they wanted to. In a town like Macklin, however, even a person's deepest secrets seemed to seep out somehow. No one ever spoke too often of Ms. Erma and old James, but those who were around during the early years of their marriage knew the brutal truth.

The evening ended when the women finished the pecan pie. Ruthann had retired to the front room and took a nap. The day had been long, the tea strong, and the talk exhausting. They left Viola and her children to be by themselves. The one thing Viola was not was lonely. They said that she had enough children to never have a lonely day the rest of her life.

*  *  *

Henry and Dyson stepped into Blake's saloon. Henry was always glad to get away, even for a few hours. Dyson had to be dragged away from Linda, practically kicking and screaming. He gave in though because Linda wasn't feeling well, and he thought he might as well. Linda wasn't crazy about him going carousing with Henry, but at least he would be out of her sight for a while. Emma had gone with Annie and Earlene over to Viola Taylor's house, so Linda could get some much-needed rest.

The men met up with Ron Craw and "Limping Larry." Blake's was set off to itself behind a wood briar patch. The women in Macklin rarely came to Blake's except women who were like the legendary Shirley Brown. It was rumored that Viola Taylor frequented the place pretty often too and that Limping Larry was the father of the last child. The bar was dark and smelled of dirt, tobacco, and cheap liquor. There was an old man named Clifton who played a fiddle. He was known to tell stories of the days when he was a slave and the many battles he had won against white folks.

This particular night though, Blake's was thick with stories from the younger men. Limping Larry, who got his name from his strange hobble, slurred his words and spit through his teeth every time he spoke.

"Yall know ah done left bout half a dozen women cause they jest didn't understand me?"

"What didn't they understand bout ya?" Ron was anxious to know.

"They thought jest cause ah limp that ah was supposed to be some kinda cripple. They didn't want me to do nothin' on my own. They was always wanting to do this or that for me."

"Man I can't hardly see nothing wrong with that." Dyson begged to differ. "Shoot, I only gat these three fingers on my hand, but Linda sho don't treat me like I'm simple. She still want me to do everything for her and then some."

"That Linda is a special case." Henry said half laughing. "Hell, she thank her butt is sweeter than the glaze on a donut."

"Well I don't know bout that, but it's pretty sweet to me." Dyson said the words and stuck his chest out a little.

"Well if she all that, why ain't you married her yet?" Limping Larry said with a twist of his head. He talked and swayed to the music playing in the background at the same time.

"Cause she don't want to get married. I done asked Linda more times than I can count. But she just don't want to that's all. Anyway, she still married to that guy in Chicago." Dyson sounded unsure, even to himself.

"Well a piece of paper ain't never stopped you before. You and Millie never jumped no broom either." Ron laughed.

Dyson hated when people mentioned Millie. When she left him, he didn't leave his house for a week. The old biddies in town had a field day. Ms. Erma and Ms. Odessa had invented every version of Dyson's last confrontation with Millie. In the first version, the two of them were in the house and it was day time. In the version that followed, they were outside of church and it was night. One version had the two scuffling on the ground and another had them fussing and cussing with Millie holding a knife to Dyson's throat. All in all, there was only one thing that had happened for certain. Millie left.

"Man I don't want to talk about that woman. I'm talking about the only woman I love and that's Linda." Dyson hiccupped.

Henry threw the last of his gin to the back of his throat. He let out a grunt to release the sting of the strong liquor.

"Don't seem to me like you loving her the right way." Henry slurred. "I mean long as we talking…"

"What you mean?" Dyson couldn't wait to hear what Henry would say next.

Henry fidgeted a little, and limping Larry decided to do a little dance to clear the air. He twirled about to the music, and Blake's seemed to come alive.

There was a short, stout woman who Limping Larry grabbed up to dance with him. She wiggled her full bosom in his face and twirled around in circles shaking her bottom. She wore a tight black dress with butterfly sleeves. Her hair was in a pin-up and she smelled of lilacs. They called her Sassy Flo. She was known in Macklin to be a carefree woman who could drink any of the men under the table. But what she really liked was just having a good time. She had a mysterious scar on her forehead that people talked about, too.

Limping Larry yelled for her to strut it and she kept on dancing. Everybody in Blake's was cheering the two of them on as they danced and sweat ran from their bodies. Dyson had not forgotten about Henry's last remark, but he was able to push it to the back of his mind. Ron grabbed up a woman himself and began doing the Lindy Hop. The entire tavern was filled with music and it seemed as if the roof would come right off the place.

Henry didn't dance, but he clapped his hands and enjoyed the music. He used to sing and play the guitar with a little band in Macklin at Blake's from time to time, but when he married Annie, she had made such a fuss about it that he had pretty much stopped. Earlene had convinced Annie that she shouldn't want a husband who had women "shakin' their tails in his face every other night."

Dyson wanted to dance with one of the Broom twins but remembered that Linda and Luella Broom's husbands were the meanest men in town. They would kill somebody over their women. Nobody ever understood why because of the way the Broom twins looked.

Henry just kept tapping his feet to the music and tossing back the gin. By the end of the night, Blake's had quieted down just enough for Dyson to hear the cars outside scatter away. In the July night, the air seemed to suffocate people as soon as they walked outside. Everybody was tipsy and had a stagger to their walk. Dyson drove since he was the only one who could actually walk a straight line. He was anxious to get home to Linda. He loved the very thought of her.

Dyson dropped Henry off and started toward the door of Linda's shack. She had refused to move in with him, even after Emma was born. She said that she was comfortable just where she was, and that if they were going to live under the same roof that it would be when she was good and ready. Dyson spent many a night at Linda's house, and she slept at his place occasionally.

Although Dyson wrestled with a secret of his own in the back of his mind, he couldn't help but think about the words Henry said at Blake's. The way Henry cocked his head and said boldly, *Don't seem to me like you loving her the right way.* He thought Henry to be out of line, but he hadn't said anything. What did he know about his and Linda's love life anyway? He couldn't shake the bad feeling he had even as he crawled into bed beside Linda. He rubbed her full belly and couldn't help but wonder just whose baby was moving around inside of her?

# 15

When the war ended, everybody danced in the road barefoot and kicked up the red earth under their feet. Lucy didn't lose either one of her sons because they had gone away to college. They both wanted to be doctors, so they had gone to live with one of Ron's well-off uncles up north. Ron and Lucy lived alone but never really had an empty house. Lucy watched Emma while Linda and Dyson went into town. Ron would joke to Lucy about having another baby, and Lucy would always say, "Man I'm forty-something years old. Ain't nothing else coming out of here!"

The two of them lived in a small house on rented land. Lucy had always said that she wanted more for her boys than a little shotgun house on somebody else's property. She pushed them to get an education, even when Ron demanded they quit school and help work the land. Lucy convinced Ron to hire out because she swore to draw her last breath the day her sons ever became farmers.

Lucy was twirling about in the kitchen when Ron stepped inside.

"Woman you finish cooking yet?" Ron yelled from the back of the house.

"When I'm finish cooking man, I'll call out to you. I ain't called out to you yet have I? Well alright then."

Lucy was always challenging Ron on something. They were convinced that they had been married for over twenty-five years because they argued so much. Even when Ron was just being himself, Lucy would always challenge him. Ron had a thing about never spending money on a Monday. His philosophy was, *If I spend some money on Monday, I'll be spending money all week.* It seemed foolish to Lucy and she would never hesitate in telling him so.

She would tell Annie about Ron's crazy habit.

"Child you can't get that man to spend a nickel on Monday."

"Sho nuff?"

"Every bit a truth in it. He thinks if he spend it on Monday, he'll be spending it all week. Now how the hell you gone *keep* spending something you ain't got?"

"But what if yall run out of something on Monday?"

"Then we'll be out til Tuesday."

"Ain't he ever bought nothing on a Monday?"

"Not long as I knowed him. Even got his sons thinking the same ole crazy way."


Annie and Lucy had gone to town to Pike's. They were shopping when Annie asked Lucy about a name that she had heard most of her life.

"Lu, just who was Shirley Brown?"

Lucy smelled a grapefruit and shook her head.

"Why you asking about that woman?"

"Cause I want to know. All I ever heard was that she was so terrible and wanted to jump in the bed with everybody's husband. And... mama accused Linda of being something like her."

"Shame on Earlene for comparing her own child to the likes of that scalawag. Girl, Linda ain't a thing like her in the least bit." Lucy smiled and shook her head. "Linda was just always free. Now I know folks done talked her in the ground, especially since she done had two babies with no husband. But trust me when I say, she ain't nothing like that Shirley Brown."

"I just don't understand why she would do that." Annie argued. "Dyson wants to marry her and she ain't thinking bout marrying him and nobody else. Now something's just wrong with that to me. A man is good enough for you to have his nappy-headed babies, but not good enough for you to marry him?"

Lucy put a can of tomato paste in her basket.

"Seem to me like it's bothering you bout Linda and Dyson not being married more than it's bothering them. Why you so concerned bout it? Honey Linda gone probably marry that man, she just givin' him a hard time or maybe she won't – either way it ain't nobody's business."

"I just thought that when she come back from Chicago things were gone be different for Linny. Instead she come back here and hopped right in the sheets with Dyson and didn't bother to marry him." Annie got close to Lucy's face and looked around the store to make sure there were no ears leaning in close.

"Plus I done heard some folks talking bout Emma not being Dyson's child. And Lu you know as well as I do that child don't look a thing like Dyson." Annie shifted her basket from one arm to the other. "I done tried real slick like to get Linny to talk to me bout it, but she ain't saying a word."

"Annie, why you saying this stuff bout your own sister? I thought…"

"You thought what? That we was close?" Annie wiped the sweat that had formed on her head away. "We are close." Annie searched for words. "I guess I never understood why she turned out so different."

"Well that's just fine. But you need to talk to your sister and at least try to understand her."

"Lu you know I done tried. You know how excited I was when she wrote that she was coming home from Chicago. I was hoping and praying that we could be close again like when we was girls." A look of disappointment blanketed Annie's face. "But that didn't happen. She just won't talk to me... not bout *that stuff* anyway."

"What you mean, *bout that stuff?*" Lucy mimicked Annie's last gesture.

"Well she won't talk bout private things, you know like men and... sex. I done told her bout Henry and me, but she won't talk bout her and Dyson, her and that Eddie, or her and nobody."

Lucy laughed.

"Girl, I for one can say amen to that!" Lucy let out a boisterous full laugh, and put her arm around Annie. "One thing you ought to learn in this life Annie is that you ain't got to tell nobody your business. For one thing, folks gone just as soon make up what they don't know bout you anyhow, and another thing is that what you and your man do between them sheets of yours is between you, him, and the good Lord."

"But we sisters Lu."

Lucy stopped and snatched Annie around to her and looked her straight in the eye.

"Now you listen to me this day. I don't care who it is. Don't *ever* tell nobody everything that go on in your house." The intensity in Lucy's eyes made Annie uneasy. "Even if it is your sister, mama, cousin, auntie, or dog – they don't need to know how Henry is giving it to you. You understand me?"

"Yes ma'am." The age difference between the two of them would surface at times, and Annie felt like she was being chastised by her mother.

Lucy continued, "If you ask me, that's why most of the non-sense go on in this town as it is – folks sleeping with one another husbands and wives and such. Now how long have you knowed me Annie?"

"Uhh..."

"Too long for you to even remember, I know. But long as you have, you ain't never heard me tell you bout me and Ron's personal business. I love you like you my own, but I ain't gonna tell you and nobody else *everything* that go on under that little roof of me and Ron's." Lucy let go of Annie's arm, and straightened her own dress. She wiped her forehead with the back of her hand and told Annie about the coming and going of Shirley Brown and how she was glad that Macklin would never see another woman like that again.

"Now I ain't gonna lie to you," Lucy's voice trailed off a little, "That Shirley Brown got a holt to my Ron, and that hurted me. But Ron Craw saw a side to miss Lucy he never thought he would see. But everything got to be alright again." Lucy shook her head.

They got back to Lucy's house and Annie helped her start her dinner. Lucy whistled while she shucked corn, and Ron came into the kitchen uptight.

"Woman, why you whistling in this house? You know that's bad luck."

Lucy ignored Ron and winked at Annie. Ron continued.

"You ought to know that a whistling woman and a crowing hen…"

"Will not come to a good end." Lucy mocked Ron and finished his sentence. "Man get on out of here so I can finish dinner. I ain't got time for your ole wives tales today. And you see somebody sittin' at this table, open up your mouth and speak."

Ron waved his hand at Lucy and nodded his head at Annie. He went back out the door.

"Now you see what I have to put up with from that ole crazy fool?" Lucy chuckled. "The other day he heard a hen crowing like a rooster and he went out and shot the thing."

Annie couldn't help but laugh.

"Yeah, I done heard daddy say that same thing before. He ain't no better. He will have a fit if somebody ate peanuts in his car. Chile don't you eat no peanuts in daddy's car right now today!"

"Lord, what he thank gone happen?" Lucy barely got the words out.

"Heck if I know, shoot. Same thing that'll happen if a woman whistle and a hen crow like a rooster I guess."

"Um hmm. Absolutely nothin'!" They laughed loud and hardy.

Annie went home and finished her own dinner. Henry still hadn't come back from Baker County. He told Annie he had to go there to get some pine wood for the outhouse door. She had asked him why couldn't he get it from Pike's but he had said that a store in Baker County had the best. So she waited up for him until it was late. She and the children ate dinner and she sent them to bed. She didn't mind Henry going out every now and then, but when he came home drunk from Blake's one night she was not happy.

It reminded her of when her father would drink and come home and fight with her mother. She knew that Henry would never raise his hand to her, but she still didn't like his drinking. One night he had come home from Blake's smelling like a distillery and still wanted to crawl between her legs. She reluctantly gave in to him, but the next morning she slammed the cabinet doors and shuffled the silverware a little louder than usual.

Henry finally walked into the house and Annie's sleepy eyes tried to focus on the blurred image coming through the door. She had fallen asleep in the front room waiting for him and ready for a fight. But now the fight had gone out of her, and she just wanted to know why it had taken him this long to get back from Baker County, which was just twenty miles or so away.

"Henry, you know what time it is?" Annie slowly rose from her chair.

"I know it's late and I'm sorry. Let's just go on to bed baby."

"Let's just go to bed?" Annie put her hand on her hip and stepped back from Henry just to make sure she had heard him right. "Henry what's goin' on with you? This time you had to go to Baker County to get a piece of darn wood. Last week you and Dyson had to go out to the Winston place to look at a car, which Dyson didn't know a thing about when I asked him. He said he had been working til late that night. Then the week before that it was something else. I can't take this no more Henry. Seem like ever since Isaiah been born, you been a different person."

Henry stood quiet. He looked at Annie and wondered why he had done this to her. She was a sweet girl and had never been touched by another man before him. She was devoted to him and only him, and he had taken her for granted. Annie was right; Henry had been deceiving her. Be that as it may, Henry still couldn't bring himself to say the words.

"I'm talking to you Henry! Don't just stand there like some deaf mute!" Her arms were swinging and she was trying to scream quiet like to keep from waking the children. "I said I'm talking to you!" Annie slapped Henry on the face. She quickly yanked her hand back and tried to shake the sting from her fingers. Henry still said nothing. He turned around and walked into the bedroom.

Annie stood there in a stunned silence. She had hit her husband. Maybe she was dreaming and this did not happen. Her throbbing hand was just a vivid trick from a bad dream. Henry had not been lying to her. No. Henry would never do it because he promised to love her always. She sat back down in the chair and lay back trying to piece things together in her mind. After a while she had come to one conclusion. Henry was seeing another woman. Of that she was certain. Her mind began to wander. He had been spending some time around his brother's wife Roxy who was friends with Sassy Flo. Could it be Sassy Flo?

There was a catch in Annie's throat like she was trying to swallow yeast. Her tears slid past the corners of her mouth and lapped under her chin. She started to doze off in the chair thinking of Viola Taylor and the fatherless baby she'd just had. This made Annie even more tired, and she didn't want to think anymore. She just sat there with her eyes fluttering as her thoughts went black.

# 16

Ruthann was weak from her night's sleep. The sun was just starting to make its debut when she turned over in her bed. She heard a rooster struggling to crow from the depth of the coop. She slowly sat up from her bed rubbing her legs that constantly ached these days. Her 97 years rarely showed signs of betrayal, but she complained of a few things in her body now and again. She no longer got on her knees to thank God for letting her see another day. Her knees were too arthritic for that now. Nowadays she looked up toward Heaven and whispered a, "Thank you Father for seeing fit to let these ole eyes see a day I ain't never seent before." Her next move was a push off the bed and a, "Thank you Father for allowin' these ole legs to still carry me."

This particular morning besides her regular winter morning aches and pains, she was troubled by a dream she'd had the night before. It wasn't out of the ordinary for Ruthann to have all of Macklin writing down her interpretations of their dreams. It was a known fact that to Ruthann, every single dream meant something. If she dreamt of fish, naturally somebody was pregnant. If she dreamt of snakes, that, without a doubt, represented enemies.

One day Lucy told Ruthann that she dreamt that all of Ron's teeth had fallen out. Ruthann told her that the dream meant great disappointment. Lucy wasn't convinced, but when Ron came home upset that he didn't get a piece of land that he had wanted to buy, Lucy changed her tune. On another occasion Viola Taylor came to her and said that her oldest boy Lee Jr. had dreamt that he was driving to Heaven in a big, long white car. Ruthann told her that she didn't like the dream. Even though it sounded like a fine dream to have, a big white car couldn't mean no good. The next week, Lee Jr. drowned in the pond on Saunter's Row.

Aside from big long luxury cars, there were two other things in dreams that were a sure sign of death, according to Ruthann. To dream of raw meat or of a wedding meant death was loitering for sure.

Ruthann dreamt of Linda in a long white wedding dress with a white veil over her face. She was finally marrying Dyson. The flowers in Linda's hand were not lovely white lilies or babies breathe – they were violets. Ruthann didn't like it one bit. She got her Bible from the chest and turned to Psalm 121. She read and rocked on the bed. "Lord, please look out for that gal," She prayed. She cried to God for Linda, whom she knew was in trouble. Just the night before she had told Earlene, "Heaven is watching, and will always be a witness to what's goin' on down here."

She was worried about Annie, too. She felt in her spirit that the child was troubled. Annie didn't open up to her as much anymore, so Ruthann knew that old Satan was up to no good. She rubbed her lower back, the pain clutching tighter these days. The wrenching ache took her back in time, seemingly a lifetime ago. She thought back to the day that she'd had her first child in slavery. She was only a girl herself, barely 16, not nearly a woman. Her petite body wracked with pain as she pushed for hours. When she saw her daughter's face it was so transparent, she swore she could see right through it.

Ruthann knew that her child being born that color would mean no good. She hated with everything in her to bring a baby into the world just to be somebody's property. She prayed that God would work a miracle. When Winnie was just two years old, slavery ended. Ruthanne had met Willie by then and they jumped the broom. Before she knew it, she had given birth to four more children. Overnight it seemed that her Winnie was no longer a sweet little girl, but a grown woman.

Ruthann felt like she blinked and suddenly Winnie had married Isaiah and had Earlene and five more children. Earlene was just as light as Winnie, but her skin was not as lucid.

Still, Ruthann hated the fact that having a child by her Master poisoned her bloodline. Miscegenation to her was the beginning of sorrows for not only her family, but countless others. It turned daughter against mother and mother against daughter. She felt that it was all because a white man couldn't keep his "thang" where it belonged.

As she slowly arose from her bed, Ruthann continued to pray through her pain. However, she couldn't shake the feeling of something happening. After all, she was never wrong about these things.

\* \* \*

The train moved through Baker County and was heading to Macklin station. Ms. Erma's oldest daughter Cassie had dozed off but was startled as the train jumped. She was heading back home to visit her mother for the first time in ten years. She had left Macklin and moved to

Memphis after her father died. She ran away with Reverend Poe's son Jesse. The two of them skipping town was
the talk of Macklin for a while, but like everything else,
that whole business too, eventually died down.

Cassie rode in silence, and then focused her eyes on
a woman sitting two seats across from her in a bright red
coat with fur around the collar. The woman wore a hat
with a wide brim and had rouge on her cheeks. Cassie lifted up from her seat still trying to be sure. She blinked her
eyes a few times because she couldn't believe she was
looking at Millie Henderson.

The train stopped at Macklin station and Cassie
waited patiently. She picked the chicken she had for lunch
out her teeth and sucked for good measure.

Cassie rubbed the crust from her eyes and wiped the
creases of her mouth. She made sure that all signs of sleep
were gone from her face. Because she sat in the colored
section of the train, she and the others in her car had to wait
until the white passengers got off first. Then Cassie spotted
a man that she'd never seen before. She wondered if the
man was with Millie. She knew the answer right away
when the man and Millie walked pass each other without so
much as a word. She caught Millie looking at the same
man too, her eyes twinkled and her lips curled ever so
slightly. Cassie walked swiftly toward Millie, who had finally recognized her. Millie dropped her bags and the two
women hugged.

"Chile I can't believe you here." Cassie stood back
from Millie, admiring her clothes.

"Yeah, I can't either. Didn't think I would ever be
back here neither, but sister wrote that my daddy ain't doing so well, so here I am." Millie twirled about.

"I'm so sorry chile. My own mama done been sick too. Can you believe all this sickness going on at Christmas time? Mm, mm, mm." Cassie shook her head.

The two of them caught up on old times. Cassie told Millie that her sister Bessie lived near Dyson and his new woman. Millie hadn't heard from Dyson in all the years she had been gone. She hadn't expected to really, since she never told anyone why she'd left him. She and Dyson had never married but planned to do it. Dyson had taken good care of her and she felt secure. She remembered that Linda Hicks would flirt with Dyson but she wasn't worried about it. She had written it off as a school girl crush. Cassie caught Millie up on all the latest gossip in town.

"Yeah chile, Bessie say Dyson and Linda real tight honey." The two of them took a seat on a bench. "He ain't married *huh* neither, and she done had a baby for 'im, and one on the way." Cassie twisted her mouth to confirm that she'd just spoken the gospel truth.

Millie cocked her head to the side.

"What you say?" Millie looked puzzled.

"Yeah honey, a little girl named Emma and one on the way ready to pop any day now." Cassie loved being the first to tell Millie the news. She looked in Millie's eyes and saw what she thought was hurt.

"*He* done gave her two babies?" Millie still appeared confused. Then out of nowhere she burst into uncontrolled laughter.

"What's wrong with you girl?" Cassie couldn't help but chuckle a little herself.

"That… that woman… whoo…" Millie couldn't get the words out through her laughter.

"Who… Linda?" Cassie was confused. "What she done did?"

Millie wiped the tears from her eyes. She regained her composure and cleared the phlegm from her throat.

"I'll tell you what she done did. She done pulled a fast one on Dyson." Cassie was unprepared for Millie's next statement. "Chile that man can't have no babies."

"What?" Cassie was just as excited to be hearing news for the first time as she was to be giving it.

"Dyson was in some kind of accident when he was little. He almost died and everything. That's why he only got them three fingers on his left hand." Millie held her hand up with her pinky and ring fingers folded down.

"That plow ran him over and cut almost right through him. He got scars on that body of his in places you wouldn't believe. Anyway, that accident messed something up on his insides, and that's the reason he can't make no babies – at least that's the story he gave me. Of course I didn't *know* none of that until I wanted to get married." Millie let out a deep breath. "And that's when he told me."

"So you just left him?" Cassie's downcast face didn't show any signs of amusement.

"Chile I was in love with that man, and I don't care what these folks in Macklin say. It broke my heart when I found out I could never have his children. He couldn't understand why I didn't want to stay, but what was I gonna do? Stay here and marry him and end up some old dried up thang and never have no babies? Shoot, *I* wasn't barren; he was the one who had the problem. I couldn't do it Cassie." That night came rushing back to Millie suddenly, and the memory wiped the smile from her mouth. "I just couldn't."

Silence engulfed them both as they sat there on the bench at the train station. They looked at the handsome strange man again. They just watched him as he sat his bag on the ground and lit a cigarette. His hair was sandy brown, and his eyes were the color of green marble. They looked at each other and then back at the man. He finally looked over at the two of them and walked in their direction. The closer he got to them, the better he looked. He took a drag on his cigarette and looked around. He wore a slick gray suit with a slim gray tie and a white shirt. He smelled like fresh soap and tobacco. His voice was as equally mesmerizing.

"Excuse me ladies." He had a slight southern accent, but sounded very proper to the women. "Would either one of you know a Linda Hicks?"

Cassie stood from the bench.

"I reckon I might." She flirted without shame. "And er uh, who might you be?"

The man picked a piece of loose tobacco from his lip and licked the place where it was.

"I'm Eddie. Eddie Rankin."

# 17

Christmas time in Macklin was always a joyous occasion. Earlene found herself knitting like crazy for her grandchildren. She would always make them a little something around the holidays. She was even making something for Linda's baby, due any day now. Ruthann declared it to be a boy so naturally nobody ever said anything to the contrary. Linda thought about naming the baby after Jeb, but Earlene wasn't having it and said that she never liked it when people named babies after old folks. Annie had already named her boy after Earlene's father whom Ruthann despised. Even though it was a coincidence, Ruthann still didn't like it. Earlene told Linda to name him something different like Erwin, or William. Still, Linda decided to wait until she saw the baby to give it a name.

Ruthann had come out of her room and Earlene took extra care with her these days, even though she was as feisty as ever.

"Mama – you alright this morning?"

"Yeah, I'm makin' it alright." Ruthann gave a straight answer without any sarcasm or smart remark. She didn't appear to be herself and Earlene immediately began to worry.

"Mama are you sure you alright?" Earlene's face was turned up. "You movin' kind of slow this morning."

That's when the Ruthann that Earlene knew well showed up.

"Well what you want me to do? Turn cartwheels across the floor gal? I'm 97 years old. I can't cut the fool every time I move."

"Mama I know that." Earlene helped Ruthann to a chair. "I'm just trying to help you woman, now stop fighting me here?"

"I'm sorry baby." Ruthann rubbed her legs again as she sat. "It's jest that ah don't feel right in my spirit today. You gat one dawta over there going out huh mind cause she done discovered that she married to a plain ole ordinary man and not some savior. Then you gat another dawta over there done gat huhself pregnant not once but twice by some..."

"I don't know what you want me to do mama." Earlene interrupted. "My girls is grown, and I can't tell 'em what to do no more than a snake can walk upright. I done all I could to bring 'em up the right way."

Earlene covered Ruthann's legs up with a multi-colored quilt and gathered wood for the stove. She started breakfast and talked as she went about the house.

"Annie ain't doing so bad. She jest figured out that a Moss man is a Moss man after all. Tried to tell that hard-headed gal that but she wouldn't listen."

"And what about your other dawta? Huh?" Ruthann talked toward the kitchen. "Ain't she none of yourn too? Seem like you never cared one way or the other how that chile gettin' along. Don't you thank that's why she up and wanted to lay with every man this side of Caleb County?" Ruthann continued. "Then you had enough nerve to compare her to the likes of Shirley Brown and run huh completely outta town. I don't call that good motherin' at all. You sho didn't learn that from me."

Earlene walked out of the kitchen and looked at Ruthann. All she could do was shake her head because the right words wouldn't come fast enough. She slowly tried to say something.

"And another thang," Ruthann continued, "You thank that chile feel good bout huhself after you done treated huh like she some lost trollop? That gal never could help huh color and you know it. Onliest reason you as bright as you is, is cause some white man thought he would sooner kill over and die if he didn't get to what was 'tween mah legs." Ruthann was rarely the sentimental type, but she poured her heart out to the grandchild she had reared.

"Gal, sometimes it grieves me to know ah done lived to see the day you was possessed with the spirit of hate for your own chile." Ruthann rubbed her legs under the quilt. "You made a difference tween them gals from the time they was born. Annie was always your sunshine and Linda was your cloud. She took huh dark color from huh daddy's peoples, so you ought to knowed better but you didn't."

Beads of perspiration started to dot on Ruthann's forehead. She reached in her bosom for her handkerchief and wiped her forehead.

"Ahm burnin' with fever in the middle of winter, so ah know mah days is numbered. Ah jest have to tell you that a person liable to do jest about anythang to get the love they feels they deserve."

Earlene stood over Ruthann's chair and finally spoke after being stunned to silence.

"Mama I tried my best with both of my girls. Linda just always seemed to fight me on every hand. That gal always did have a head like stone."

"Ain't gat nothin' to do with it." Ruthann coughed a dry, soft cough. "Ah hope the Lawd let you live to see your mistakes." She got up from her chair and put her feeble arms around Earlene. "Baby, all ahm sayin' is that you gat to make thangs right tween you and Linda. Heaven knows that she ain't no angel, shucks. And I know cause Heaven knows and done tol me all its secrets. That gal gonna need somebody Earlene." Ruthann's voice was like a declaration. "She gonna need some*body*."

*    *    *

"Mama, that man comin' up the road with some pecans and candy!" Hester ran from the window to Annie in the kitchen. "You said you was gonna buy some today." She ran around the kitchen table, her bare feet slapping the wood.

"I done told you bout runnin' around this house with no shoes on cold as it is. Now get on out of here!" Annie started baking her pies two days before Christmas just like Ruthann had always done. "Take this nickel and get Isaiah to go out in the front with you." Hester took the nickel. "And put some shoes on your feet!" Annie yelled at the child's back.

Ms. Odessa promised to come over and help Annie with her chocolate cake recipe. She met the children in the yard and came up on the porch. Ms. Odessa was 70, but she was still pretty. She had married one of Macklin's most prosperous farmers in her day, and they had three sets of twins. The first set she'd had were fraternal twins, a girl and a boy. The two sets that followed were identical twin boys. She would always say that God had smiled on her because she only had to be walking around with a big belly three times instead of six. She and her late husband, Zeb, had five sons and one daughter. The daughter was the oldest and came out the tiniest.

All of Ms. Odessa's children had had something peculiar about them. The first set of twins, Leah and Lincoln, were born with birth marks on their foreheads. They were shaped like strawberries because Ms. Odessa said she craved strawberries the whole time she carried them. The middle twins were Isaac and Jacob, named because she had gone into labor during her weekly Bible study. The last sets of twins were John and Jethro, who never grew to be over five feet tall. Ms. Odessa never failed in explaining the boys' height by saying that she had laughed at old Mr. Townsend for being the shortest man in all of Mississippi. So she knew she had "marked" her babies when they wouldn't grow past the age of ten.

After Zeb died and the children moved out and away, Ms. Odessa took to minding everybody's business but her own. She took the opportunity of telling the whole town that Paul Jessup's soul was burning in hell for having a heart attack on top of Shirley Brown. His widow, Margaret, never acknowledged Ms. Odessa's comments but didn't completely ignore them either. Margaret Jessup had even released her anger on Annie in Pike's not long before when she'd spat, *That Ms. Odessa jest as two-faced as a double-headed penny. And if she think I don't know she was the one spreaded that lie bout my Paul and that Shirley Brown, well she jest as blind as a bombat!* Annie never commented, but she knew that Margaret was so deep in the river of denial that she needed a fishing rod to drag her out.

Ms. Odessa walked into the kitchen where Annie was starting her chocolate cake. She had been cooking all morning and Henry was out once again.

The children came in from outside with their candy and pecans. Ms. Odessa didn't even sit down but started to help Annie immediately.

"Chile let me show you how to do this one good time. My own mama used to make these cakes and I never forgot it."

Hester and Isaiah walked into the kitchen crunching candy in their teeth. Hester walked up to Ms. Odessa, looking her up and down before walking a full circle around her.

"Girl what is you lookin' for?" Annie said with her hands on her hips.

Hester looked puzzled and asked Annie, "Mama, I thought Ms. Jessup say she had two faces."

Annie was too embarrassed to say anything, so she shooed Hester and Isaiah out of the kitchen.

Ms. Odessa didn't crack a smile and never said a word.

"You know how kids is Ms. Odessa." Annie nervously stirred the cake batter. "I don't know where she done picked up…"

"I know jest where she picked it up." Ms. Odessa slammed a spoon down on the table. "To think I nursed that woman back to health when she grieved herself sick over that bed hoppin' dead husband of hers." She tossed her thick hair back over her shoulder. "I ain't never felt so foolish in all my life."

Annie wanted to ease the awkward air in the kitchen. So she tried her best to steer the subject away from Paul and Margaret Jessup. She also thought about just how she was going to tear Hester's behind up as soon as Ms. Odessa left.

"Ms. Odessa, where Ms. Erma at today?"

Still feeling a little betrayed, Ms. Odessa answered with caution.

"Well she ain't feeling so good, so her children there trying to comfort her some. Cassie done came here from Memphis to see bout her mama too."

"Cassie?" Annie hadn't heard her name mentioned in so long. "She still married to Jesse Poe?"

"Chile she still married to that piece o' man." Ms. Odessa was back to herself again. "Humph, you ask me, she ain't too right in the head. What kind of woman will run away with the preacher's son, then run around on him like it ain't no tomorrow?"

"Now Ms. Odessa, you shouldn't be saying that." Annie couldn't believe her nerve.

"I'm just telling the truth. Seem like folks around here don't know the meaning of that word. My Zeb always said I would stand on truth even if it would kill my mama." She closed her eyes like she was proclaiming righteousness.

"Well I don't know and I ain't trying to get in nobody's business." Annie knew she didn't want to get on the subject of husbands, especially since she saw less and less of Henry. "I got a man of my own that I'm trying to keep in line."

Though Annie felt that she might regret opening up the subject to one of the biggest gossips in town, she had to get it off her chest.

"Ms. Odessa, you ever seen Henry around Viola Taylor? I mean... have you ever seen him going to her house?" Annie immediately regretted mentioning it, but it was too late to take the words back.

"Chile, I ain't never seen him go over there, but that don't mean he ain't been that way." She sipped some water from a cup on the table. "Why you askin?"

"It's been kind of bothering me bout Henry being gone all the time and Viola Taylor done had another baby…"

"You just can't jump to conclusions Annie. You should always give a man the benefit of the doubt, least til he give you reason to take it back." She leaned in closer to Annie even though it was just the two of them in the kitchen. "You ain't gat no reason to take it back is you?"

Before Annie could answer, Sarah came toddling into the kitchen. She had woke up from her nap earlier than Annie anticipated. Annie picked her up and put her on her hip.

"Where my daddy?" Sarah sucked her thumb and rubbed Annie's curly hair with her other hand. Annie said nothing. She wasn't trying to be mean, she just didn't know the answer herself.

# 18

It wasn't that Eddie was a stranger to the south, because he had been born in Louisiana and could blend in with the best of southern gentlemen.  Macklin, however, wasn't like the place he knew.  Macklin was different from any town he'd ever seen.  There was something unique and mysterious about it, and he was anxious to see Linda.  From all of her letters over the years, he had been expecting her to meet him with open arms.

Linda was to meet Eddie at Blake's.  Since she'd had Emma, she didn't nearly frequent the place as often as she did before, but this was a special occasion.

Cassie and Millie had given Eddie instructions on how to cross the bridge and walk through thickets.  He saw Blake's tavern peeking out from behind some magnolia trees.  The air wasn't quite cold, but there was a breeze.  He'd thought that it was somehow beneath him to come to the sticks of Mississippi just to see Linda again.  She had left an impression on him, of that he was sure.  He couldn't stop thinking about her body and the way it hypnotized him.  Her smell stayed with him even long after she'd left.  His wife, Vicki, had come back to a husband who was stupid over someone else.

She was too busy with her dancing to even notice half the time.  Vicki had enrolled in a school of dance just to improve her already perfect form.  She didn't even fuss when the first letter from Linda had come that day in Chicago. Vicki knew Eddie ran around on her, and she had always without fail confronted him with fury. She would curse him and even slap him sometimes. But something about this time was different. That day, she simply gave Eddie the letter and watched as he opened it.

After that one, many followed. He continued to write back to Linda. Then, one night Eddie came in from a gig at the Blue Room and found Vicki's clothes gone from the apartment. There was no trace of her ever having been there. She didn't leave a bobby pin, a tube of lipstick, or even a pair of panties. He didn't even smell the scent of lilies, which was her favorite perfume. She was gone, and for all of about a minute he felt empty, betrayed. He and Vicki had their share of problems, but she had always forgiven him.

He couldn't explain to her though why he would go so far as to marry someone else while she was in Paris. He just knew that it felt right at the time, but it was so wrong. There was something about Linda that Eddie just couldn't do without. One night after throwing back some bourbon to ease the sting of Vicki's leaving, Eddie picked up a letter from Linda. Her words were always easy. In them, he read a longing for him. He immediately wrote her back and told her that he was coming to Macklin. Linda didn't hesitate writing him back and extending an invitation. The next thing Eddie knew he was on a train to Macklin, Mississippi.

Linda slipped on a bright yellow dress. Her stomach was stretched to its limit underneath, but she still felt the butterflies. It wasn't the baby wanting to come out, but it was the feeling she always got whenever she thought of Eddie. His train had come in this afternoon, and she was going to meet him at Blake's. He had written her and told her that he just had to see her. She didn't want him coming to her house, not yet anyway. In all of her letters, she had never told Eddie about Dyson or her child. She thought maybe because there could never really be any real chance of her and Eddie being together again.

She thought that if Eddie knew she was half-living with Dyson and had a child, he would put her completely out of his mind. She couldn't bear the idea of being a passing thought to Eddie. As hard as she tried, she had never stopped loving him. Eddie knew it, she knew it, and Ruthann knew it. Linda was simply glowing after reading one of Eddie's letters that had come one day. Ruthann let her know that she was wrong as wrong could be.

"You round here floatin' on clouds bout some man way up in Chicago, when you ought to be tryin' to walk the straight and narrow with a life fit to meet your maker."

"Granny, I ain't trying to be introduced to my maker no time soon. Besides, me and Eddie understand one another that way." Linda respected her great-grandmother, but still did just as she pleased.

"Well when somethin' up and happens on the count o' you clownin' over one man and leadin' another one on, don't say ah didn't try to tell you."

Linda admitted to herself that Ruthann's words had a way of coming true, but she couldn't think about that now that Eddie was actually here. She sprayed some Jasmine bloom perfume on her neck and rubbed the insides of her wrists in the spots she sprayed. Her mind ran rampant trying to figure out how she was going to face Eddie with her stomach as big as the side of a barn. In constant motion, Linda headed out of the house. Dyson was working and Emma was with Annie. Linda walked into the cool of the evening to meet Eddie.

Ms. Erma lay in bed sick with a fever for five days. She was glad that Cassie had come from Memphis. She loved the attention that her daughters gave her when she wasn't feeling good.

"Cassie, is that you?"

"Yeah mama, I'm here. You get your rest now, and me, Flossie and Bessie gone take care of everything." Cassie looked around the house. "Where they at anyway?"

"They went yonder to Ms. Odessa's to get some camphor for my throat."

"And it took the two of 'em to go?" Cassie's tone was condescending.

"They be right back. Chile don't come in here arguing with me now. You know ah ain't got the energy no more. Ain't enough you done shamed me and this family by running off with the reverend's son. Now you got to sass me too?"

Cassie and her mother never really agreed on much. Cassie remembered her father's violent rages as a child, and she blamed her mother for never standing up to him.

"Mama every time I'm in your house, all you do is tell me what I ain't done right. That's why I left here in the first place. You was always on me bout something. All those times I set up with you after daddy had gone into one of his fits, you would think I deserved a few kind words from you every now and then. I come all the way from Memphis not just cause it's Christmas time, but because Bessie told me you was sick. Ain't that enough mama?"

Ms. Erma sat still, thinking of how to respond. Just as she was forming her thoughts, Flossie and Bessie came through the door of the house. Each one of them hugged Cassie's neck and caught her up on the talk of Macklin.

"Sister how was the train ride?" Flossie sat down in a chair. She was plump with a wide behind that jiggled when she walked. She was the color of oak, and had a lisp when she talked. Her face was round, and she had dimples that seemed to poke right through to the insides of her mouth. She was a pretty woman, but she could stand to cut back on a meal or two, is what most people said about her behind her back.

"It was alright I guess." Cassie was still trying to calm down from her tirade against Ms. Erma. "Them old trains still the same as always – separating the whites from the blacks, which is probably the best thing *to* do. I don't hardly want to be staring in no white folks' faces no how."

"I know that's right." Bessie chimed in. "Old Dale Hinckley with his funny looking self done come back in town after visiting his aunt in Greenburg County. I reckon it's true what they say bout him. I sho wouldn't want to look in that face on no long train ride."

"It wasn't too long." Cassie rubbed her aching feet. "Yall won't believe who was on the train with me." Before the sisters could even ask, Cassie blurted out, "Millie Henderson!"

"Millie Henderson?" Flossie and Bessie said in unison.

"Sho nuff. And looking good too if I must say. And she done told me something that nigh bout knocked me out cold." Cassie was so excited to finally tell everything she had just heard. "She done come back here 'cause Mr. Henderson done took ill. She ain't been here since she hot footed it out of town when she left Dyson."

"Speakin' of hot footin' sister. Ain't you the pot callin' the kettle black? You skipped out of here yourself with Jesse Poe mind you." Bessie snickered at Cassie.

Bessie was rail thin. Cassie was on the plump side. People had always said that Cassie and Flossie looked like twins, except Flossie was lighter than Cassie. Of all the similarities between them, their color was the one difference that everybody always seemed to point out.

"Aw hush gal and listen to what she done told me." Cassie said, cutting her sister off. "She said the reason she left Dyson was because he couldn't give her no babies."

"Chile the man *was* older than her." Flossie said through a mouthful of cake.

"Honey he wasn't nearly that old. Anyway God done fixed a man to so he can shoot babies out til he wrinkled and bent over." Bessie chuckled.

"I tell you." Cassie laughed and finished her story. "He couldn't have no babies cause he was in some kind of wreck when he was a lil boy. Well everybody knew that part on the count of them three fingers he gat dangling there on his hand. But Millie say that the accident messed something on his insides up the reason he can't make no babies."

"Sho nuff?" Flossie and Bessie sang in unison.

"Mmm hmm. And she say she just couldn't stay down here married to Dyson and never have no children. She done had two little boys since then she say. So I say God bless her."

"What the devil is going on then?" Bessie demanded from her sister. "I'm the one that wrote and told you that Dyson and Linda Hicks was playing house and having babies." Bessie had helped Cassie rub her feet. She threw Cassie's foot to the floor. "What you trying to tell us gal?"

"I'm trying to tell yall that Linda Hicks done come up pregnant not once but twice. And accordin' to Millie,

Dyson know full well them babies can't be none of his. And if he know it, Linda sho as hell know it too."

The sisters continued to talk in hushed tones, careful not to disturb Ms. Erma. They knew she was sick and didn't feel well, but they also knew that she was one of the nosiest old women in Macklin.

Ms. Erma was in the next room dozing off to sleep. She heard her daughters talking but was too weak to comment or get excited. She knew that what she had just heard was going to shake Macklin in ways it hadn't been shaken since Shirley Brown came to town. She dozed off to sleep wondering what all of Macklin would soon be asking. Who was the father of Linda's babies?

*     *     *

Eddie swooned to the music at Blake's and was surprised that such a small town knew good music. Blake had been watching Eddie from the minute he came through the door. Blake thought that he looked pretty classy, at least compared to most of the men he saw in Macklin. Most men who came into his place wore a hard day's work on their faces. This stranger looked like he had never seen a hard day's work in his life. Blake dried the same glass in his hand over and over, making sure to keep his eye on the man.

The waitress was a short, squash colored woman with a tiny waste and wide hips. She wore ruby red lipstick and bangle earrings. She always had a few drinks herself before she started her shift at Blake's. She knew she wasn't supposed to, but Blake never put up much of a fuss about it. She switched over to Eddie and made sure she stood close enough to him so he couldn't miss her ample bosom.

"Hey now. What you drinkin?"

"I'll take some scotch, seeing how it's still early." Eddie smiled at her, revealing his perfectly straight teeth.

"Comin' right up honey." She turned to walk away, then quickly turned back. "You ain't from around here." She got closer to Eddie and rubbed her hip against his suit. "What blowed you this direction all the way from…"

"Chicago." Eddie finished her sentence. "And I'm here to meet an old friend. Well, a special friend."

"Who might this friend be? It's a small town and I'm sho to know her." The waitress instantly assumed the special friend to be a woman. She searched Eddie's eyes for any contradiction.

"Indeed you might. Do you know Linda Hicks?"

"I sho do!"

In his mind Eddie questioned the excitement in the waitress's voice.

"Well then that's who I've come to meet." He pulled a case from his inside suit pocket, pulled out a cigarette and lit it. "I'll take that drink now."

"Comin' right up." The waitress hurried out of his sight.

Smoke filled the tiny joint, and Eddie relaxed in its laid back atmosphere. The haze made him feel like he was dreaming. His impatience for his drink emerged in a tapping of his foot to the music. He looked up and saw the waitress and smiled.

"Here you go honey." She tried to sit the drink on the table in front of Eddie, but he intercepted it before it hit the wood.

"Thank you kindly. How much do I owe you?"

"Just enjoy yourself and see me before you leave." The waitress fanned herself with her hand, still smiling at Eddie. "I'll be here all night."

"Thanks." Eddie tossed half of the scotch down his throat and sat back in his chair. He would certainly need to be in an altered state to see Linda eye to eye again. If she still had the same effect on him she had five years ago in Chicago, he knew he had to brace himself. He emptied his glass and sat still for a moment.

The musician in Eddie always took over when he was buzzed. He closed his eyes and commenced to playing an imaginary saxophone.

He was deep into his jazz number when he was interrupted by a tap on his shoulder, and when he turned around, he was almost blinded by yellowness. Eddie focused and looked up into a pair of eyes. He was suspended there for a moment and was fooled for a split second by her trance like gaze. His eyes slowly rolled downward and he realized that he was looking at a pregnant woman.

"Linda." He said her name because he hadn't said it back to her since that last day in the apartment in Chicago. He said her name out loud, and yet he didn't feel as if he was addressing her. He said her name.

"It's me Eddie." Linda twirled about for him. "It's all me."

Eddie rubbed his eyes, but couldn't make the rest of his body do anything else.

"Ain't you got no hug for me baby?" Linda stretched her arms out. She suddenly realized how ridiculous the whole thing was and the smile dropped from her face. Right away she knew that she had to explain.

"I know I didn't tell you." She fidgeted with her purse. "I... I just didn't know how that's all. I thought the baby would have come by now, since it was weeks ago when you wrote that you was coming. Anyway I knew you loved the Linda that you remembered, so it didn't matter to me that I wasn't that girl no more. In our letters we would *always* be how we remembered."

Eddie motioned for the waitress and she scurried over to the table.

"Keep 'em coming," was all he said.

She ran back and got him another drink. She had met Linda at the door a few minutes before and couldn't help but to tell her, "Girl, you gat a fine thing waitin' on you right over there."

Linda had taken one look around the tiny place and spotted Eddie instantly. She didn't know how to hide herself or even be ashamed of her circumstance. She simply strutted across the floor as her belly led the way. Now she stood before the man she had loved for so long and pregnant with another man's child.

"Linda you have to excuse me, but this is the very last thing I expected." Eddie rubbed his temples. "Here I was all set to come and rescue you from the sticks of this mud hole you call a town, and you've picked up right where you left off."

"What the hell is that supposed to mean Eddie?" Linda didn't feel like she had the right to defend herself, but her voice couldn't hide it.

"I mean two weeks ago I wrote you and told you that I was coming here, and I thought you knew why. Now how the hell am I supposed to whisk you off into the sunset with you knocked up with some other man's child?"

"You wait just a minute. I know I *should* have told you, but I didn't. You was the one married." Linda paused before continuing. "I got another little girl at home and she's almost three years old now.  I love my child and I'm gone love this one too.  I'm gone be having it any day now."  Linda rubbed Eddie's head.  "We can still be together.  That's why I come over here."

"Woman – you out of your mind!"  Eddie lit another cigarette.  "I don't know what you got all planned out, but count me out of it.  I plan to be on the next thing smokin' out of this backward town."

"Eddie listen to me."  Linda tugged at Eddie's arm. "Can you at least listen to what I got to say?"

Eddie blew smoke in the opposite direction of Linda's face.  He figured he had come a long way and the least he could do was listen to her story, however absurd it may sound.  He wanted to do the noble thing and just listen.

"Alright baby.  I can't wait to hear this one."

Linda positioned herself in the already uncomfortable chair.  She rubbed her full belly, and let out a deep breath.

"Eddie I wanted to tell you but I thought you wouldn't want me if you knew I been with somebody else."

"But you should've let me make that choice."  His voice was loud enough to turn heads in the tiny place.  "Instead I have to come way down here just to see you with your belly sticking out from being knocked up by some…"  Eddie managed a chuckle.  Not because the situation caused for outright laughter, but because in the grand scheme of things, it was a little funny.

"I can see why you would be mad at me.  I don't even blame you for it."  Linda's eyes glistened with tears.  "But when your… wife came back, I didn't know what else to do.  You hurt me baby… but I still love you.  I know it's crazy, but I do.  Spite of what went on here."  Linda rubbed her stomach.

"So this is how you repaid me huh? *I'll show that bastard. Let me invite him here like I love his dirty drawls, and oops surprise! I'm pregnant!* Eddie twisted his face as he mocked Linda and what he thought she had conspired behind his back.

"That ain't how it came about and you know it." Linda wiped her tears and stood from the table. "But if you want to go on back to Chicago with them kind of thoughts roamin' in your head then I can't stop you."

Eddie smashed his cigarette butt into the ash tray. There was silence for a moment as he watched Linda prepare to walk out of his life for good. He had felt in his gut that Linda wouldn't be just sitting around waiting for him. She was far too beautiful of a woman for that. Sitting around pining over a man wasn't for nobody like Linda. That kind of thing was for ugly women and old settlers. He finally stood too, looking down on Linda and still admiring the fire in her eyes. He tilted her tear-stained face upward and slowly moved his own face down to meet hers. He kissed her lips, savoring the sweetness that he'd dreamed about for years.

Linda didn't put any emotion into her lips. She knew that if she put one drop of energy into kissing Eddie back with passion, she wouldn't be able to stop. She began to cry again, this time she sobbed without control. Eddie put his arms around her, but Linda pulled back.

"Eddie go on and leave me alone. Just go on and get out of here."

Her sudden fury tore at Eddie's heart. He looked at Linda and she knew that he wanted to know what had come over her. So before he could even ask she answered.

"You don't want to love nobody like me anyway. I done something that I should be ashamed of. But I know you the last person to feel sorry for me any kind of way. So just go Eddie – it's the best thing anyway."

"What have you done?" Eddie asked out of true concern.

"Something so bad that if I died today, I don't think God or the devil would want me."

"Linda, please. What is it?" Eddie searched her eyes for something, but her eyes had turned cold.

"I deserve anything that I got coming to me."

"Does somebody want to hurt you? Tell me!" Eddie demanded. "I'll kill anybody who tries to lay a hand on you." He surprised himself with the anger that flew from his lips.

"Bye Eddie." Linda quickly walked out of Blake's.

Eddie wanted to run after her, but he fell back down into his chair, and banged his head on the table in rapid movements. This sent the waitress running over to him.

"You ok sugar?"

Eddie slowly lifted his head, his bloodshot red eyes half closed.

"No. I'm not."

"Is there anythang I can do for you?" The waitress rubbed Eddie's face with the back of her hand. "You just name it sugar."

"Sure." Through his pain, Eddie managed to give the waitress a smile that made her knees weak. "You can tell me where I can find the daddy to Linda's baby."

The waitress sat down and rubbed Eddie's hands. He charmed her long enough to get the directions to Dyson McCloud's place. Then he was gone.

# 19

Earlene was making some curtains for Reverend Poe's wife, Alice. She was known in Macklin for having God blessed hands that could do wonders with a needle and thread. She made all of her own clothes as well as Annie and Linda's when they were little girls. These days her eyes were getting a little weak, so she had a lamp lit even though the sun hadn't quite set yet.

Ruthann was asleep and Earlene had sent Jeb over to Ms. Erma's with some chicken soup. Earlene heard the door rattle and looked up expecting to see Jeb. It was Linda, who stumbled a little as she came into the door, and Earlene knew right away that she was in trouble.

Linda slowly walked to a chair and sat down. Earlene could see that she had been crying. She had learned that when her daughters came to her this way that she would wait for them to speak so as she wouldn't be prying. She continued her sowing and just waited.

"Mama?"

"Mmm hmm?" Earlene never looked up from her needle and thread, although she was fretting inside.

"I don't feel good. I…" Linda's eyes rolled up in her head, and her lids fluttered.

Earlene dropped her curtains in progress and ran to Linda. She fixed her mouth to call for Ruthann who was already walking into the room.

"She ain't ready to have this baby and somethin' done upset her." Ruthann touched Linda's forehead then ordered Earlene about. "Well don't just stand there help me lay huh flat."

"Mama is she gonna be alright?" Earlene asked Ruthann childlike.

"This gal gonna be just fine. Soon as she can forgive huhself for what she done."

"Mama you think she that upset for having children without being married? I don't know why this gal insist on doing things so backward." Earlene fanned Linda and looked up to God and hoped that her cry for Him to forgive her child was heard.

"Chile where a new life is concerned, God done already forgive us." Ruthann rubbed Linda's head. "This chile got worser sins that need to be pardoned."

Linda attempted to speak, but her mouth slurred every syllable.

"It's alright, mama's here baby." Earlene whispered in Linda's ear.

Through her daze Linda could hear Earlene's voice. The sound stroked her at her very core. Her whole life she had heard Earlene speak to Annie with this voice, but never to her. In the midst of the pain of her contractions, she was moved by another power. Earlene had finally spoken to *her* in a mother's tone.

The room seemed to close in on Linda as her breathing became more and more labored. "Am I gonna die mama? I can't die, not before I…"

"No baby, ain't nobody dyin' today." Earlene began humming "Jesus Loves Me" softly.

*　　*　　*

Eddie staggered to the door of Blake's and looked in both directions. He realized that he had come too far to

be defeated by some backwoods bumpkin with a name like
Dyson McCloud. He had the piece of paper folded in his
suit pocket with Dyson's name and address on it. He was
determined to win Linda back. Maybe she was right –
maybe she could have the baby and leave town with him.
Since she was still pregnant, however, he knew that wasn't
possible. Eddie was hoping for something.

He walked into the road and didn't know what to
expect when he met this other man face to face. Eddie
pulled out his pocket watch and checked the time. It was
five past six and the sun was slowly setting. He asked himself over and over how he ended up chasing down a man in
the country over a woman who he could never have.

He neared Dyson's farm and slowed down. The
placed looked very well kept in comparison to a lot of other
places that he'd passed on the way. He saw two cars in
front of the house, and the land was at least a couple of
acres long. It was all fenced in, and Eddie started to wonder now if Linda wasn't too bad off. If she was with a man
who owned all of this, what would she want with him?
Eddie started to wonder if the man Linda was pregnant by
was a white man. Then just as he got closer to the gate he
saw a man walk out of the door and head for the barn. He
ducked behind a tree and watched.

He knew right away that the man wasn't white. The
man actually looked fairly strong and had a swagger to his
walk. He was kind of tall and had a medium build. Eddie
looked around the place and questioned the man's intent
with Linda.

He couldn't be angry at this man for having someone like Linda. After all, he did lie to her in Chicago and
had broken her heart. She had come back here and hooked

up with this man, who from the looks of it could definitely take care of her.

Eddie watched as the man came out of the barn. The man looked worried and fidgety. He walked back into the house, and Eddie wondered what Linda saw in him. He wasn't a bad looking man, but he didn't look anything like what he thought was Linda's type. He assumed that Linda's taste in men would be half as good looking as he was. He wondered if Linda was inside and if they were about to sit down to dinner. He forced his mind to stop wandering as he stood behind the tree and gathered his thoughts as well as his nerve.

*      *      *

Annie had waited for Linda to come back from town for hours. She had fed the children and put them to bed. She thought Emma might as well stay the night, especially if Linda was going over to Dyson's. It wouldn't be the first time she'd left Emma there, so Annie tried not to worry. But with Linda's baby due soon, she hoped that nothing had happened.

Annie kept looking out of the window over to Linda's house to see if a light had come on. The little place was still dark. She waited and wondered what happened, and she also wondered where Henry was – again. She heard a car drive up and she immediately ran over to the window, thinking it was Henry. Her eyes narrowed to a squint as she focused on the figure that emerged from the car. It was her father and he seemed to be in a panic. Annie ran to the door and yanked it open before Jeb got to the porch.

"Daddy?" Annie ran toward Jeb in a frenzy. "What's wrong? Is it Linny?"

"Yeah chile." Jeb knew that Annie thought the worse. As if to put his daughter at ease, he smiled. "When I got back from Ms. Erma's place, your sister was there and she was fixin' to have that baby. Mama told me to come here to let you know since Emma been here with you."

"Thank God." Annie fell back in a chair on the tiny porch. "I liked to died worrying bout that gal. Least I know she ain't in some ditch somewhere."

"Indeed." Jeb noticed Annie's uneasiness and sensed that something else was wrong. He hated to butt into either of his daughters' business, but the father in him just couldn't help it at times. "Is everything else alright Annie?"

In that instant Annie became a little girl again. She thought about the time when Bubba Bailey hit her when she was seven, and she had come running home to tell Jeb. Her father had always seemed to chase the bad out of her life. She wanted Jeb to come to her rescue again. This time it was Henry, and she felt lonely most of the time because he was never home. The children were constantly asking where he was, and Annie wanted to give them some answers. Annie wanted Jeb to hold her and tell her that Henry was just going through something that all men went through, and that he was still in love with her. But instead of telling Jeb any of this, she simply answered with a low voice,

"Yes sir. Everything alright." She feigned a smile. "Just a little tired that's all. I'm just glad Linny alright," Annie lied. She switched the tension away from her and Henry. "Is Dyson over there with her?"

Jeb left things as they were, and he didn't press Annie for anything more. He still knew that something else was bothering her, but he wasn't one to pry. He simply answered her question.

"Naw, he ain't there. I stopped by his place but he didn't seem to be home neither. I thought it was kind of strange since that car of his was out back, but I just left it and come on here."

"Aw he probably out with Henry drinking at Blake's or somewhere. That would be my guess daddy. They'll probably be on back soon. I tell him then."

"You want me to go over to Blake's on my way home to see if he's there?" Jeb really wanted to go by Blake's to tell Henry to get home to his wife, who was worrying herself sick over *his* hanging out to all hours.

"No daddy. Thanks anyhow." Annie stood up from the chair to let Jeb know that she would be fine once he left. "You get on back to the house now cause they might need you to do something else. You know how them two women get."

Jeb chuckled.

"Ok by me baby." He kissed Annie on the forehead. "I see you later hear?"

"Ok daddy."

Annie watched Jeb as he drove off in the distance. She was startled by the front door opening behind her.

"Mama, who was that?" Isaiah rubbed his eyes as he stumbled onto the porch in the darkness.

"That was your granddaddy. And you should be in the bed boy. Come on back in here." Annie grabbed Isaiah's frail arm and pulled him back in the house.

"Your sisters and Emma trying to sleep, and here you are walking the floor."

"I gotta go mama." Isaiah switched his weight from each foot.

"Why didn't you tell me that before we came back inside boy?"

Annie yanked Isaiah's arm and headed out the door. She fussed all the way to the outhouse.

"I done told you a million times to go *before* you get your tail in the bed. Now here every night you taking me and your daddy through this same mess."

"Sorry mama but I just ain't have to go before I got in the bed. I try to make myself have to go, but I can't." Isaiah pulled up his pajamas while Annie patted her foot.

As they headed back toward the house, Annie noticed the front door sitting open. She stopped in her tracks yanking Isaiah back in the process. She knew she had closed the door behind them.

"What's wrong mama?"

Annie shushed Isaiah and stood frozen in her tracks. Someone was in the house with the children. The night air seemed to get even colder as every horrible thought came to her mind.

"Mama, I'm scared."

"I said shut up boy." Annie watched the figure through the window going from room to room. "Isaiah you stay right here and don't you move."

"But I'm scared out here at night mama. You know that."

"I ain't got time for your nonsense boy. Stay right here and don't you move!" Annie put the fear of God into Isaiah and tiptoed through the grass and onto the front porch. She was afraid, but her fears aside, she knew that her children and Emma were in the house with some stranger. As she stepped into the house, she screamed and almost fell back.

"Henry!"

"Of course it's me baby. What you doing? Where is Isaiah?" Henry was just as startled to run into Annie.

Annie ran back onto the porch and called for Isaiah. He came running up to the house as fast as his tiny legs could carry him.

"Mama/ I was scared/ and I heard something back there/ and I heard you call me/ and I just ran!" Isaiah panted and paused between every other word.

"Come on in this house." Annie said in relief. "It was just your daddy." Annie turned her neck from Isaiah to Henry. "Henry where your car? I'm going out of my mind thinking somebody was gone run away with these children and all the time it was you creeping round here. What's going on with you Henry? Is some other woman driving that car?"

Finally, Annie could no longer hold her peace concerning Henry's disappearing acts. She had made up in her mind that she was going to get to the bottom of it that night if it killed her.

"I'm talking to you Henry," Annie hollered, unmoved by the fact that she might wake the children.

"Naw ain't no other woman in my car Annie. You talkin' nonsense. I wish you would stop nagging me bout everything all the time."

Henry realized that he owed Annie an explanation for his not being in the car, but his mind wasn't working fast enough to please her. There was no way he could tell her the truth about what really happened, not now anyway. He thought about telling her that somebody had stolen the car, but there was no one in Macklin who would steal from a Moss. So he told her something that would soothe her ears, for tonight anyway.

"I guess I had a little too much to drink tonight at Blake's so I had one of the boys drop me off on Starch Road. My car still at Blake's and I can get it tomorrow. Now let's just go on to bed."

"You ain't gettin' in my bed tonight and not no night til you tell me the truth." Tears stung Annie's eyes. "Do I look like a fool to you man?"

"Mama…"

"Shut up Isaiah and get back to bed." Annie snapped.

Isaiah ran into the bedroom. Annie continued to empty her fury on Henry.

"Henry I never thought when I married you that you would be just like your brothers. You promised me better and I believed you. Now here I am raising these kids half-way by myself, and all you can do is lie to me?"

"Annie I don't mean to hurt you, but I'm just a man and I can't say I'm no better than nobody else when it comes to different things. Just love me anyhow honey cause I still love you even if I done made some mistakes."

The house was still and the night wind whistled through the floorboards. Annie wiped her face with the back of her hand and walked away from Henry. She suddenly remembered that she still had something to say.

"So that's it? You been runnin' around on me and you want me to just love you? What the hell do I look like Henry a doormat? Who is it?" Annie's voice lowered to almost a whisper. "Who is it I asked you?"

"Annie."

"It's that loose hipped heffah Viola Taylor ain't it?"

Henry was silent. He decided it was better that he said nothing and let Annie finish painting the picture in her mind.

"It don't matter honey cause I'm done with steppin' out on you. Baby I know this thing done hurt you and I'm sorry as a man can be." Henry grabbed Annie and pulled her into him. He kissed her on the top of her head and squeezed her as tight as he could. "Please find it in your heart to forgive me Annie. You the onliest one I love... I know that now."

Annie felt trapped in Henry's embrace, but she didn't put up a fight. She stayed cuddled there and listened to his heart beating. She wished that she could judge his sincerity by the beats of his heart. She wished.

# 20

The morning sun peaked from behind the hills that bordered Macklin. All seemed quiet and peaceful, and the innocence of a new life had brought much needed joy. Linda had been in labor all night and had given birth to a boy just before dawn. Ruthann said that it was a sign when a baby was born at the darkest part of night. She said that when a baby comes into the world with such excitement and expectation, there would certainly be a test of faith soon to follow.

Linda was still weak from the hard delivery, so Ruthann and Earlene had demanded her to rest. She woke up mumbling and coughing, trying to get her words out clearly. Earlene walked up to the bed and put her hand on Linda's forehead.

"Shhh. Don't you try to talk chile. You done been through enough."

"Eddie," Linda called out with her eyes still closed. "I got to see Eddie."

"What you talking' gal?" Earlene stood over Linda with her hands on her hips. "You mean to tell me you still studyin' bout that man in Chicago? Chile you need to be thinkin' up a name for this here little boy you got. He a fine boy too. Dyson gonna love him to death."

"No mama, Eddie's right here in Macklin." Linda threw the heavy blanket from her legs and twisted her body in position to get out of bed.

"Gal don't make me call your grandmamma in here, now sat yourself down! If that Eddie is in town the best thing for him to do is to go right on back where he come from. Last thing you need is some man coming here and sending you through some kind of fit. No wonder this baby come here early - upsettin' yourself over some man." Earlene had lost the gentle streak she'd had at that moment. "Now just lay on down here and rest. I done sent your daddy over to Dyson's to let him know the baby done come."

Linda grabbed the covers and slid them back over her body. She thought about Dyson and immediately became sad. Her tears were real, but she didn't know exactly who she was sad for. She thought about her new baby boy and how she never meant to hurt Dyson. She promised Dyson that if it was a boy that she would leave the naming to him. She laid her head back on the pillow thinking that everything that she'd been trying to hide for so long was about to come out.

*       *       *

Jeb headed out of the house as demanded by Earlene. He had held his new grandson in his arms and wondered how the years had passed him by. He had always wanted a son of his own, but when God decided to give him two little girls he didn't complain. He looked at the baby and decided that he looked like Linda and maybe even him a little. Just like Emma, this baby didn't resemble Dyson a bit. But Jeb knew all about family genes and how odd they were.

His own daughters were two different shades. Linda took after his side of the family and Annie took after her mother.  Over the years he wished that Earlene would have given Linda as much attention as she did Annie.  He had always felt closer to Linda because they shared a common bond.  Although Jeb isn't considered "dark," he didn't really mind that Earlene was a light skinned woman when he married her, but he also knew that being light was better than being dark in the South.

Jeb had made it his business to make Linda feel loved.  It hurt him deeply when Linda started seeking love from everywhere else.  He never approved of her going around with men, some even his age and older.  He never voiced his disappointment because he felt that Linda had been through enough growing up.  Instead, he continued to be as good a father as he could, even if it meant he had to keep his thoughts to himself.

As he neared Dyson's farm, he decided that he was going to have a long talk with Dyson.  The least a man could do is marry a woman who was having his babies.  He recalled Linda going on about not wanting to marry Dyson, but that was never good enough for him.  Jeb wanted the best for both of his girls, and if being married was going to keep Linda from hopping around, then so be it.

Dyson's yard was empty except for a few chickens roaming about.  The barn door was open, and it looked as if Dyson had skipped his morning chores.  Jeb walked up to the house and onto the porch.  Oddly, the front door was cracked, so he slowly stepped inside.  He knocked on the open door to be polite and even called for Dyson a few times.

The front room was in disarray and the curtains were still pulled from the night before.  Jeb felt his knees weaken as he continued walking through the house.  He called for Dyson several more times and still there was no response. Jeb turned the corner of the front room into the kitchen. Sunlight streamed through the clear side of a window that was otherwise thick with film and dust. As he neared the table, Jeb let out a gasp.

Dyson lay on the floor by the table, his body as still as a piece of wood. His eyes were open as if they were looking to the sky. His hands were balled up into fists. In one of them he was holding a leather case of some sort. There was a hole in his chest and blood had run all over the floor, clear through the kitchen.

Jeb put his hand to his mouth and backed away from Dyson's lifeless body. He wondered who would kill Dyson in his own house and just two days before Christmas. He wondered what Dyson had in his hand. He was so shaken up that he didn't bother to touch Dyson or anything in the house. He ran out of the house to Ms. Odessa's place, which was just down the road.

Before Jeb could get to the house, Ms. Odessa saw him running toward her. In the winter time, she was always looking out of the window watching people as they passed by. She spotted the crazed look in Jeb's eyes and she immediately came running out of the house. Jeb got to her porch and was out of breath but somehow still managed to get his words out.

"Ms. Odessa – something terrible done happened!"

"Slow down chile. Now what is it?"

"I just come from Dyson's place to tell him that Linda done had the baby. When I got to the house, I found him…" Jeb paused to catch his breath, "He was just as dead as he could be – right there on his kitchen floor. Somebody shot him! Blowed a hole right through him!"

For once Ms. Odessa was speechless. She stood there with her mouth open and a blank look in her eyes.

"Ms. Odessa we got to get the law and…"

"Don't you worry bout it now. You just go on back
home and let Earlene and Ruthann know what done happened. Try not to upset Linda with this now – poor thang.
I don't know what she gonna do without a daddy for them
chillun." Ms. Odessa sounded sincere to Jeb, but in her
mind she was thinking about who she could get the news to
first. "I'll send the lil Baker boy for the law. Now you go
on."

Jeb ran back down the road toward Dyson's farm.
He wondered if he should go to Annie's and tell her and
Henry about what had happened. He knew how close Hen-
ry and Dyson were and that Henry would be upset.
Anyway, he figured Ms. Odessa would do the job and tell
the whole town by the time he got back home.

\*       \*       \*

Millie had slept so sound in her mother's house.
When she was a little girl, she felt safe in the comfort of her
home. Then her sister married Mr. Sims and moved him
into the house and her life changed drastically. Since she
had left town, she had not been back to Macklin for any
reason. She met and married a wonderful man and had two
sons. Even when her sister wrote to her about what was
going on back home, she didn't want to return. She had
heard about births, deaths, marriages, and all kinds of mis-
haps, but the only thing that got her back to Macklin was
her father's illness. Besides her parents and sisters, there
was no one else in Macklin whom she cared that much
about. She questioned that thought though whenever Dyson ran across her mind.

There was a time when Millie loved Dyson to no end. She had actually wanted to marry him and have his babies. They lived together for two years before he told her that he couldn't have children. It broke her heart to leave him and Macklin, but she did it anyway. Christmas time was always so different in Macklin. Everyone seemed to be in the spirit of giving and good nature. Any grudges that were being held against anyone were always put off until after the holidays.

This morning had been good despite her father's ailment. She was going to help her mother and sisters finish making the sweet potato pies and pound cakes. Christmas was two days away and the old excitement of the joyous time had filled her heart. This was the first time that she had been away from her own children for Christmas. Her husband told her to go and see about her father, so she hopped a train and came back to the one place she would never forget. She had planned to see to her family and enjoy Christmas and head right back to Little Rock, Arkansas.

The house was warm and smelled sweet. Her father was getting better and everything seemed to be going according to her plan. Millie had no desire to see or speak to anyone else in town. She thought about Dyson and Linda and how Dyson had to know that Linda was sleeping around and popping out babies that weren't his. Maybe they had an arrangement that was just known between the two of them. But she put her thoughts to rest. She decided that Dyson was no longer her problem and hadn't been for years now.

She continued her Christmas rituals and sang and laughed with her sisters. Then there was a knock on the door. It was Ms. Odessa, who would come to visit her mother every now and then. She wondered who or what the latest gossip was about this time. Ms. Odessa was always in somebody's business, and Millie knew that this morning couldn't have been any exception.

"How you doing today Ms. Odessa?" Millie asked in a playful way.

"Chile I'm doing alright. But I'm afraid I got some bad news for yall this morning."

For the first time, Millie's family saw a serious look in the old woman's eyes and believed that what she was about to say was also serious. Ms. Odessa helped herself to a chair and began crying before she could tell them the story.

"Ms. Odessa what is it?" Mrs. Henderson asked out of frustration.

"Well, Jeb Hicks just left here not long ago and he told me that he had been to Dyson's place and he found him there dead."

The room expanded with sighs and gasps from the women.

"I sent the lil Baker boy for the law and to tell Annie and Henry on his way."

"Dead? Father help us." Mrs. Henderson always had a prayer on her lips. "Was he sick? How did it happen? Was Linda and the baby there?" The questions flowed from Mrs. Henderson.

"Jeb just say he was shot. That's all I know. It sho is a shame. "Lawd have mercy!"

After answering the door, Millie went back to pouring sweet potato filling into the pie crusts ready to go into the oven. After hearing what Ms. Odessa said, she stood there with dough still clinging to her fingers. Her body went numb and she fell to the floor. Her sisters ran over to her and lifted her head. Millie hoped that she had just imagined the last thing that Ms. Odessa said. This could not be happening. How could Dyson be dead? She knew that only one thing could have happened. Millie began to play a scene of Dyson confronting Linda about the babies in her mind. Linda had to have gotten angry and did the unthinkable. At that moment, Millie was convinced that Linda had killed Dyson.

*　　　*　　　*

Jeb got back to the house and felt his heart sink at the idea of having to tell Linda about Dyson. He couldn't understand why God would allow something like this to happen around Christmas. But then he knew better than anyone else that death had no respect of persons, or respect of time. His own mother had died on Easter Sunday, a holiday that he never fully enjoyed after that.

Jeb slowly walked in the house and walked into the kitchen. Earlene was still sowing and cooking at the same time. The baby was with Linda in the next room. Ruthann was in the parlor napping as always.

"Jeb, is that you?" Earlene called from the kitchen.

Jeb didn't answer. Instead, he walked into the kitchen where she was and stood there.

"What is it? Where is Dyson? Didn't he come with you?"

Jeb walked over to Earlene and sat in a chair next to her.

"Honey I got something bad to tell you… Dyson… Dyson can't come. Somebody done shot him."

"What? What you saying? Is he alright?"

"Naw. He dead Earlene." Jeb flinched, and tried to shake the sight of Dyson lying in his own blood out of his head.

Earlene dropped her needle and thread. As she screamed and cried, Ruthann came in from the parlor. Jeb dropped to his knees and buried his face in Earlene's lap. He grabbed her around her waist and held her. Ruthann walked over to the two of them.

"What's done happened?"

Jeb turned his face from Earlene and told Ruthann the news. Ruthann slowly turned back around. She didn't seem moved in any way. They both looked at her and wondered what was going on in her mind. She walked away muttering a few words. They couldn't make out what she was saying.

"We got to tell Linda… and we got to go see bout what happened to Dyson." Earlene was shaken up, but she still wanted to get to the bottom of things. Although she never approved of Dyson and Linda's relationship, she would have never wished such tragedy on him, nor her worst enemy.

"Ms. Odessa sent for the law and I'm sho Annie and Henry done heard by now." Before Jeb got the words out good, Annie and Henry came through the door with the children. Annie was still crying and Henry had Sarah in his arms.

"Mama we heard what happened. Is Linda alright?"

"We ain't told her yet. Y' daddy just got through the door good." Earlene's voice was monotone.

"Well somebody got to tell her." Henry commanded.

"We'll tell her soon as she wake up. Right now she and the baby is resting. Don't come in this house raising your voice Henry. I think we know what to do at a time like this." Jeb's words came like fire at Henry. He didn't appreciate lip from Henry at all these days, especially since he knew that he had been running around on Annie.

"I'm just saying Jeb that I think that the woman got a right to know that…"

"Like I said, we gone tell her when *we* get ready. Now Henry, take them children and go on in the front room."

Earlene was surprised by Jeb's reaction. He was never the one to take charge or raise his voice, not since he had stopped drinking. Annie looked at Henry and her eyes confirmed what Jeb had said. Henry took Sarah and Isaiah into the front room. Hester had already skipped to the parlor to see Ruthann.

Annie spoke, still crying.

"Mama I don't know why somebody would do something like this. Henry said that he was alright yesterday, just had a little too much to drink at Blake's is all. Henry is just sick over it."

"Baby it ain't no tellin' why people do what they do, but I sho hope they catch whoever did this. I ain't never been crazy bout Dyson, but it grieves my heart to know somebody shot him down like a dog in his own house."

"So Henry was with him yesterday?" Jeb asked Annie.

"Yeah, he said they was at Blake's and they both had a little too much to drink. Henry say that David brought him home cause Dyson had already left."

"And you know this for sho?"

"Well that's what Henry said daddy. That's all I know."

Ruthann came into the kitchen with Hester at her heels. Silence entered the house yet again. Suddenly the quiet was broken by a door opening. Linda walked into the kitchen with the baby in her arms.

"Hey Annie, yall come to see my little strong boy?"

"He so little." Hester ran over to Linda. "Can I hold him?"

"Not yet baby. Let your mama hold him first ok?" Linda handed the baby to Annie. She noticed the tears in her sister's eyes. "Annie what's wrong?"

"You need to be resting gal," Earlene snapped. "Don't you ever listen?"

"Ain't no need for me to be cooped up in no room all day – shoot I only had a baby."

"Don't you get sassy gal. You almost left here tryin' to have that boy – now you need your rest!" Ruthann still had authority in her voice, although she too was a bit frail these days.

"Alright, alright I'm going. Guess I can't argue with that."

Henry walked back into the kitchen and stood next to Annie. He looked at the baby and asked what his name was.

"Well I ain't thought of no name for him yet. I promised Dyson that if it was a boy that he could give him a name."

Everyone became quiet. They knew that Linda's next words would be asking where Dyson was. Earlene thought that maybe Linda was too dazed and weak to re-member that she told her that Jeb was going to get Dyson. Henry wanted to speak, but Annie grabbed him by the waist and pulled her to him. No one said a word. What shocked them more was that Linda took the baby from Annie and walked back into the room without another word. She never asked about Dyson.

*     *     *

Millie and Cassie had been old friends. After what she had told Cassie at the train station, Millie wondered how far the word had gotten. If she was lucky, Cassie had only told Flossie and Bessie, and they hadn't told their husbands. If she wasn't lucky, everybody in town had known that Dyson didn't father Linda's babies. When Ms. Odessa came to the house that morning and told her the news about Dyson, Millie was convinced that Linda had killed Dyson. She couldn't tell anybody else of her suspicions except the one person she told her secret to in the first place. She knew that if Linda did kill Dyson, she stood to get everything he had.

Even though they weren't married by law, Millie knew that Dyson must have loved Linda enough to leave everything to her. Even though Millie was married now with her own life, she couldn't stand by and let Linda get away with killing Dyson for his money. It was clear to Millie that Linda wanted to run off and marry the real father of her children. Millie hoped that she was wrong, but she knew that she needed an ally to back her up. She had been gone from Macklin too long to tell anybody else, so she could only think of one person.

Ms. Erma had recovered well from her illness. She started to help Cassie, Flossie, and Bessie with the cooking for Christmas. Everyone in town had always had their cooking done before Christmas Eve service at church. The house smelled of ham, potato salad, turkey and dressing,

and collard greens. Ms. Odessa had already told them
about Dyson. Ms. Erma had told them that God didn't
make no mistakes and that they had to keep on keepin' on.
They would go over to Linda's and make sure she was alright. The rest of that morning they talked about Linda and
Dyson and the babies. By then, Ms. Erma had let her
daughters know that she heard them talking about Dyson
not fathering Linda's children. As they talked the rest of
that day, there was a solemn mood. The knock on the door
had surprised the women as they picked at the food.

Cassie answered the door, and Millie yanked her
outside and onto the porch.

"What in the devil?"

"Shhhhh." Millie closed the door behind Cassie
and looked at the window of the house to make sure no one
was looking out at them. "I come to tell you something,
but you have to promise me that you won't tell your sisters
and especially your mama."

"What you talkin' girl? My mama and my sisters
already know about Dyson not being the daddy of Linda's
babies. But they ain't gonna say nothing."

Millie gave Cassie a look of disbelief. All in a day,
Cassie had come home and told Flossie, Bessie, and Ms.
Erma what she had told her at the train station. It had taken
her a while to remember the kind of town Macklin was.
Suddenly, Millie knew that she was home.

"Cassie, remember when I told you that Linda was
gettin' those babies from somebody else cause they
couldn't be Dyson's?"

"Mmm hmm. Of course I remember. Shame that
man had to go to his grave and not know the whole truth. I
mean, I guess he knew they couldn't be his, but he still had
the right to know who they did belong to..."

"Well anyway," Millie interrupted, "I think I know what happened."

Cassie's eyes got bigger and her mouth started to salivate at what Millie was about to say.

"What girl? What you know?"

"I think Linda done killed Dyson for his money. I think she want to go off and marry the real daddy of them babies."

"You really think Linda can do a thang like that?"

"Honey my mama always said that a woman will do bout anything when she love a man. And don't you re-member that fine man at the train station askin' bout Linda?"

"Mmm hmm I sho do." A smiled crossed Cassie's face. "Hard to forget a man who look like that. Shoot, I think I would kill somebody myself to be with a man like him." Cassie chuckled.

"Cassie this ain't funny. Dyson is dead! Now I know he wasn't no saint. Hell, he kept me hangin' on to him for two years before he told me he couldn't have no babies. But he darn sho didn't deserve to die for it."

"Ok, ok. What you tellin' me all this for? And how you know Linda did it for sho? Anybody could have killed Dyson, much mess as he talked to folks. He always did think he was better than the rest of us just cause he owned a lil piece of land." Cassie turned to walk back into the house. "Chile, a thang like this don't happen in Macklin, but I ain't the one to try to say who did what."

"Cassie I'm tryin' to talk to you. Don't you believe nothin' I'm sayin'?"

"Look-a-here – it's a sad thang. Christmas is in two days, and the Eve service is tomorrow, and…"

"Never mind all that!" Millie waved her hands. "I'm sorry I come here." Millie turned to walk off the porch. "Just forget I ever said anything. But if Linda up and leave town all of a sudden, you just remember what I done told you."

Millie walked off the porch and Cassie watched her in the distance. She wondered if what Millie said was true. She thought about the handsome man at the train station. She even wondered if a man who looked as good as he did could kill somebody. The more Cassie thought about it, the more confused she became. In all of her years in Macklin she had never known of anybody ever being killed in their own house and left like a raccoon on the side of the road. It was 1946 though, and these days anything was possible.

# 21

David Moss had been at Blake's the night before against Roxy's wishes. She, just like all the other wives in Macklin, didn't like the type of women who hung out at Blake's. Linda used to spend a lot of time in Blake's before she moved away and went to Chicago. David remembered his many trysts with Linda before she moved. He even promised to leave her alone after Roxy found out and told him that she would leave him. Then she threatened him with the words, *If I hear-tell of you ever talking to that spook Linda Hicks again, so help me I will kill you dead David.* After that, David focused his affections on other women in the town, including Viola Taylor.

Even still, David could never forget Linda's smooth skin and her ample breasts. And in spite of Roxy's threats, he still enjoyed a few romps with Linda every now and again. It angered him at times that a man like Dyson was even touching her. A man who was just shy of being an outright cripple himself was laying it to Linda. David never really felt guilty about his actions. He thought that Roxy should have known what she was in for when she married a Moss man anyway. He knew that she, just like the rest of her sisters-in-law, was smitten. David was the best lover she'd ever had. Roxy had only been with two other men, and they both paled in comparison to David, and she never let a night of sex go by without telling her husband so.

After Henry had been drinking his troubles away at Blake's, David figured it was over some woman, and not Annie. He and his brothers shared their many stories about the women in town that they had conquered.  They traded sex tales like collectible baseball cards.

That night, David had told Henry that he had to get home to Roxy.  The next day Roxy told him that Dyson was found dead with three bullet holes in his chest and a stab wound to his head.  In Macklin, by the time word got around town, the truth had been turned around five different ways.

Roxy said that the lil Baker boy had told everybody in town after he went to the sheriff.   The coroner had already gone to get Dyson's body.  Roxy reminded David that it could have been him shot up and cut up.  She knew that he still messed around with every woman in town, including Linda.  David didn't respond at the news.  He figured that a woman as gorgeous as Linda could do much better than the likes of Dyson anyway.

*          *          *

As the day grew on people all over Macklin had heard about Dyson.  Murders in Macklin were rare.  There was hardly ever a strange killing for miles around.  Whenever a man turned up dead there were only two things that he could have died for in a town like Macklin; gambling, or over some woman.  Annie was sick about Dyson and cried most of the day.  She never handled death very well.  When she was little, she would cry every time Jeb killed a chicken or a pig on the place.  It didn't matter who or what died, Annie took the loss personal.

She kept telling Henry that it just wasn't right for Emma and that baby to not have a daddy.  As upset as she was, she kept thinking over and over in her mind about Linda.  She helped Ruthann and Earlene with Christmas dinner and tried to keep her head up. They were all in the front room in front of the fire. Finally, Annie couldn't take anymore, and she let her anger loose on the family.

"Don't yall think it's time that we go in there and tell her that that baby's father is dead? How long we gone walk around here and keep something like this from her? She got to know, and I'm going in there to tell her."

Henry grabbed Annie and spun her around.

"You ain't gonna do no such thing. Don't you think it's mighty strange that she didn't even ask about Dyson? I mean all the day long she in there resting with a baby with no name cause she waitin' on Dyson to name him. But she ain't even asked about him. She couldn't have loved him *that* much. Something just ain't right."

"No Henry, somethin' ain't right." Ruthann butted in. "And it ain't been right for a long time." Her voice was full of force, and when she spoke like this everyone knew that a "Heaven's Eye's" was coming next. "That gal been hurtin' most all her life 'cause she ain't never felt loved the right way."

Ruthann stood in the middle of the front room and walked slowly in a circle. "I know you tried to do right by her Jeb and maybe that's why she ain't as bad off as she could be. But Earlene, you mistreated that gal for her color ever since she been in this world. I done seed it, and everybody round here done seed it."

Earlene tried to speak, but Ruthann cut her off and turned to Henry.

"And you. . ." Ruthann turned to Henry. "You gat yourself a pretty wife, and yet and still you 'lowed the devil to trick you into carryin' on like your daddy and beddin' every woman in town. And if you ask me, you deserve whatever you got comin' to you boy. But it ain't for me to judge you cause God the onliest one can do that. Heaven knows and tells me all its secrets. And I may not be round to see everythang come to pass, but Heaven's got eyes and is watchin."

Annie cried even more. She knew that Ruthann would not be in the dark about Henry's running around on her. She'd hoped that after his apology the night before that things would be different. He promised her that his days of tipping out on her were over. He was done, and he loved only her. She wanted to believe him more than anything. Now it broke her heart to hear Ruthann say those things about him. He was still her husband, and if she chose to forgive him, she couldn't let anybody, not even her great-grandmother, whom she loved and respected, to say anything bad about him. After all, he was the father of her children, so quite naturally she jumped to Henry's defense.

"Grandma I know that Henry ain't been all the way right with me for the past few years, but he still my husband. He ain't never let me and these children see a hungry day. He would rather see his own self dead before he let that happen. He been a good provider for me, I love him, and I'm gone stand by his side."

Earlene and Jeb didn't say anything. Instead, they listened to Annie defend Henry and they wondered why she was protecting him. Even when Annie would be crying to them because Henry was coming home late at night, they never once told her what to do. Jeb would tell her that she had her own life and that she should pray about it and ask God to help her. Earlene never failed in giving Annie the *Moss mens ain't worth a snaggle tooth cat* speech. But Annie stuck it out and confided in Lucy Craw on the days when she felt like she would break.

Henry sat there with his head hung down. His mother had raised him to never disrespect his elders, and he never did. He knew that what Ruthann said was true. He didn't know why he did what he did, but he hoped that God would forgive him. He was proud that Annie stood up for him, but at the same time he was ashamed.

As the quiet engulfed them once again, Linda came out of the room and said that she was hungry.

"I'm starving. Ain't nobody gonna have some of that potato pie?"

No one said a word. Earlene dropped her head. Annie's eyes glistened with tears, and Henry looked away. Ruthann sat there almost stoic. Finally Jeb stood up and went over to Linda. He walked her into the kitchen and whispered.

They heard her crying, and Annie sobbed all the more. Earlene ran into the kitchen to comfort Linda. Henry ran after her and then caught himself and ran over to Annie. Ruthann sat in her rocking chair and hummed an old hymn.

The next sound that was heard was a screeching cry from the bedroom. The nameless little boy was making his presence known, too.

By the time word about Dyson had circled around town a second time, Jeb's story about what he'd found had been twisted to no end. The coroner had reported that Dyson had been dead for about a day but was still uncertain as to how many hours exactly. The sheriff hadn't even started questioning anyone, especially since this was not the run of the mill case. Once every so often in a small town like Macklin, a man ended up dead over a gambling debt, or a domestic fight, so Sheriff Mann was baffled at something

like this. Dyson wasn't a gambling man, and Linda Hicks
was the only woman Dyson ever went crazy over after Millie Henderson had left town. Everyone knew that. The
leather case that was tucked in Dyson's hand was taken to
the station. Sheriff Mann didn't think too much about what
was in it at the time, but he was sure it would lead to something.

\*         \*         \*

Linda held the baby close to her chest. Somehow
this whole thing seemed like a dream. She had wanted to
tell Dyson that she wasn't faithful to him and that Emma
and this new baby were not his. She thought that once she
had the baby she would tell him the truth and run away
with Eddie. Only Eddie had gotten to town before the baby
was born, and she was forced to let him slip through her
fingers once again. Over the last few months she had kept
the thought of being with Eddie close to her heart. Even
though she'd cheated on Dyson with other men, there was
really only one other man that she spent most of her time
with.

She was ashamed at herself now and wished that
she could have a second chance. She felt horrible and unfit
to mother any child. As she sat there rocking the baby, she
wondered now what she would name him. She thought
about naming him after Dyson, but somehow looking into
the baby's face and seeing her lover there, she knew that
would not be right. She thought about naming him after
her father, but she never really liked the name Jebediah.

Then she thought about the only other little boy in
the family, and that he had a biblical name. She knew that
Ruthann didn't like the name Isaiah because it was Earlene's father's name, and he had abandoned her and her

siblings. However, it was biblical after all, and despite her distaste for the name, Ruthann did grow to love little Isaiah.

Linda pulled open the drawer of the nightstand next to the bed and picked up the Bible inside. She flipped through several pages and looked through the Old Testament. She passed by the names Ezekial and Daniel, and Elijah and Elisha. She skimmed over Amos and Jonah, and Joshua and David. She then remembered a story in the New Testament that she loved as a little girl. She flipped to the book of Acts and found the spot. It was the story of Paul on the road to Damascus, who was blinded and fell from his horse. He was led by a man named Ananias and was without his sight for three days. When his sight was restored, Paul was a changed man. He no longer went around hurting those who believed in Jesus, but he was converted and became one of Jesus' best soldiers.

Linda closed the book and looked down at her son. She thought about her life and what she had done in order for the baby to be here. She hoped to be forgiven for deceiving a man and doing such a terrible deed. Deep down, she had always felt that Dyson deserved a better woman than her. So in the spirit of redemption, she called her son Paul. She hoped that the boy would always be reminded that no matter what a person has done, there is always hope and room for forgiveness. She looked down at baby Paul, and staring back at her were his father's eyes.

Linda knew that she had to come clean. Dyson was dead. She now had to tell herself the truth and admit that it was all over. She knew that she would risk everything, even the love of her own family. She also knew that there was no turning back now. She still couldn't understand how both times she had conceived a child, and by some odd mystery – both times the babies were not Dyson's. The odds at how it could happen escaped her. She was hoping to see Dyson in this boy. It would somehow ease her guilt. Once again, she would have to live with it the rest of her life.

Annie went home with Henry knowing that she would be with him the rest of her life. He wasn't perfect, but he loved her and she was sure of that. She had three children for Henry, and she knew that he wanted more. She would have as many children as he wanted and be the best wife she could be to him. She had a newfound appreciation for Henry and her little family. Annie thought that it was unfortunate that Linda's children would grow up without their father, but at least hers would always have theirs. She wanted Henry to be there for Emma and the new baby as much as he could.

In all the excitement, no one stopped to ask Henry how he felt since Dyson was killed. They had been friends for years. Dyson had given Henry a job when he was just a boy, and they formed a bond that lasted over the years. When Henry had his eye on Annie, it was Dyson who told him to go for it. Henry assumed that Annie wouldn't want a man as dark as he was, but she fell for him right off. After Millie left town, Henry was there to tell Dyson that it would be alright. He went so far as to introducing him to Roxy's cousin Helen. Although it didn't work out between them, Dyson never held it against Henry.

When Linda set her sights on Dyson, Henry had his doubts. He told Dyson to be careful about falling for a woman like Linda. She might end up breaking his heart. He told Dyson that his brother David, as well as a good number of other men in town had been with her. Then just as if Henry had predicted it, Linda left town and headed to

Chicago.  She left Dyson and told him that she couldn't stand all the talk in town about her and him.

Henry had never shared all of Dyson's business with Annie.  He would always tell her that he didn't like talking about people and that Macklin had enough gossips in it to fill up two towns.  Still, Annie never felt like she was making Henry talk about people.  She just convinced him that as his wife, it was his duty to share everything with her.  After that, Henry did share most everything with Annie, except the one thing she should have been told a long time ago.

# 22

The Christmas Eve service was one of the biggest turn-outs Macklin had ever had. Even folks who didn't come near church were there, if for nothing else but to hear the latest hearsay. Since Dyson had been found dead, there was plenty of talk going around. Since he had no immediate family in town, the planning of Dyson's funeral was left up to Linda. She was ordered to rest by Earlene and Ruthann, so Annie and Henry took over the arrangements.

Reverend Poe was shocked that something like this had happened in Macklin. Just before Christmas Eve service began, he spoke about it to Ms. Erma and Ms. Odessa.

"Ah just can't hardly believe something like this done happened in these parts. Lawd knows ah done lived to see bout everythang in my day, but ah ain't never seed somethin' like this."

"Cryin' out shame if you ask me." Ms. Odessa agreed. "I ain't sayin' that Dyson was the most upstandin' citizen round here, shucks he done flounced round with more women than you can shake a stick at. And he ain't had the gumption to marry nary one of them. But it still don't make somebody shootin' him dead through the head right, no shape nor fashion."

To her own surprise, Ms. Erma hadn't told Ms. Odessa that Dyson couldn't have children. If she knew her old friend like she thought she did, Ms. Odessa would take credit for Dyson telling her firsthand himself, so she kept the secret under wraps to appease Cassie, Flossie, and Bessie. They knew as well as anybody in town that their mother couldn't hold water in a bucket.

People continued to gather in the church and there were still discussions about what had taken place, who they thought might have done it, and just how much money Dyson really had. Annie wouldn't discuss any of it with people, and she demanded Henry to do the same. She had told him,

"Folks ain't hardly had a good word to say bout Dyson while he was alive, so I sho ain't gonna let nobody talk about him now."

"He was a good man." Henry said slowly. "Can't see why nobody would say anything bad bout him at all. He helped mo folks in this town, and he never asked for nothin' in place of it. He was just that kind o' man that's all. I figures the Lawd won't make another one like him no time soon."

The service was under way and Reverend Poe stood at the front. He usually preached about Jesus and the wise men on Christmas Eve, but instead he began speaking on loyalty.

"Now ah know that by now most everybody done heard bout our dear brother Dyson. Most everybody know that ah loved him like he was my own, too."

A few hums in unison rang out over the small church. The pastor continued.

"And ah know that this ain't a time for us to be quiet on a matter that done shaken up Macklin so." He paused and his eyes narrowed to a squint. "But sho as ah'm standin' right cheer, ah know that the Lawd gonna see us through!"

The Amens climbed over the benches and met Reverend Poe where he stood.

"And ah know that whosomever did such a horrible thang to brother Dyson, gots to have a heart. So we pray to you Lawd, let this man, woman or child come forth and serve justice. And may they make the devil out a lirah and tell the truth!" Reverend Poe shouted deep from his lungs and the sweat poured from his face. People agreed with him and began to tell each other that the reverend was speaking the gospel truth. They lit candles as they always did for the Christmas Eve service and sang "Silent Night."

After the service was over, Ms. Odessa invited everyone over to her house as she did every year. She'd made her famous hot water cornbread and turnip greens. She cooked the greens with the bottoms still in them, and she swore that the greens were bland without them. She always dashed a pinch of her secret recipe that she'd gotten from her grandmother, a former slave, who was a cook for one of the presidents. She never told anybody in town what the secret ingredient was, but it tasted so good that everybody stopped caring what she did to them.

Even though everyone was invited, it was usually the same people who came. Margaret Jessup came in spite of her differences with Ms. Erma and Ms. Odessa. She said that she was coming out of respect, since it was a memorial for Dyson in a way. It was just as well that the meeting place was at Ms. Odessa's because she had the biggest house among the black folks in town. It was the home she'd raised her six children in, and she vowed to never leave it.

By the time the sweet potato pie was being served, Dyson's murder had not been discussed at all. It was a touchy subject, and oddly enough, no one wanted to offend

Linda in her absence by anything they said. Those who had the least bit of compassion for Linda said encouraging words to Jeb and Earlene. Those who had nothing but contempt for her, could never before, and not even then, hold their peace.

"So how long did they say Dyson was dead when they found him?" Viola Taylor asked no one in particular.

Everyone continued to talk among themselves. Some didn't hear Viola's question, and some chose not to acknowledge it.

"I said, how long was Dyson dead when they found 'im?" Viola's voice climbed a few octaves. This time she made sure she was heard.

"They said they wasn't for sho." David's wife Roxy answered with a smirk. "But it sho is a shame that he laid there long as he did, especially since he was *supposed* to have somebody who looked after him." Her face turned up, as her eyes darted quickly in Earlene's direction, then back to her pie.

"What?" Earlene snapped. "If you call yourself tryin' to say something you two-faced heffah, you oughta come on out and say it, stead o' hintin' all around like somebody supposed be as dumb as you are!"

Earlene's new-found love for Linda released emotions that rose to the top of her belly and boiled there like a hot toddy. She continued.

"If yall think I'm gonna sit here and let yall insult my daughter in her grief, then the both of you are jest as foolish as you look."

Jeb grabbed Earlene. "Baby come on now. Ah think it's time we get on outta here."

"Yeah you take her on home you old drunk," Roxy walked toward Earlene and Jeb, "And have a few drinks for me while you at it."

Ruthann saw what was about to unravel, and she made a decision in her mind not to say anything. Ruthann knew that this day was bound to come and the things that were about to be said were bound to be made known, but Earlene was not ready to give up the fight so easily.

"I advise you to get away from me and mine and stay away!" Earlene pointed a finger in Roxy's direction.

"Or what?" Viola chimed in. "You gonna lock us out in the cold and leave us all night?"

"Or better yet," Roxy chuckled, "sleep with your other daughter's husband?"

Earlene's face froze. She knew that Macklin was a small town and that just about everything that went on in town was never private, but how did they know about such things? She looked at Jeb, and turned and walked toward the door. Jeb followed her with a look that was a cross between bewilderment and fury.

Annie walked from the kitchen into the front room where everyone was gathered. The sudden silence had drawn her and the other women who were preparing and serving food there. Although she hadn't heard anything that had been said, the look on everyone's faces told her that something had just happened.

"What's going on in here?" She asked blankly.

"We leaving," Earlene managed with a shake in her voice. "Time we get back to the house and check on Linda.

"Is everything alright?"

"Naw, everythang ain't alright." Jeb released his anger. "These gals here bent on talkin' mess bout us and now they makin' up lies."

"Lies?" Viola held the word longer than she had to. "Ain't no lie bout how you used to drink and beat up on your wife. And ain't no lie bout how *after* those fights she fount comfort in the arms of another man. Just too bad that man layin' dead full of bullet holes now and he can't speak for hisself!"

Gasps and mumbles filled the room.

Margaret Jessup spoke up. "Are you trying to say that Earlene and Dyson?"

"I ain't *tryin* to say nothin.' I'm out and out sayin' it!" Viola shouted her last remark.

"And you stand there and think that we supposed to believe that lie, just like the one yall put out bout my Paul and that Shirley Brown?" Margaret stood up for Earlene. "I couldn't understand why my husband wanted to move back to this God-forsaken place after his mama died. Far as I'm concerned that piece of land wasn't worth moving around you bunch of hicks and your back woods ways!"

Ms. Odessa kept quiet, although she was the ring leader in telling everybody about Paul Jessup. However, she felt compelled to speak up just to try to get them talking more about Earlene and Dyson.

"Now Ms. Margaret," Ms. Odessa finally said, "Ah don't know what you done heard, but…"

"Don't you try to sweet talk me old woman," Margaret interrupted. "Because I know it was you who spreaded that lie from the git-go. And if you think your Zeb was so true and holy, honey all you got to do is open them ole eyes of yours and take a good look at Viola Taylor over there." Margaret pointed her finger at Viola. "Then maybe you'll finally see that she done had bout three babies by your dear sweet Zeb!" Margaret ended her spill with a sharp twist of her head and a wave of her hand for effect.

Ms. Odessa put her hand to her chest. Her breathing became labored and her eyes welled with tears. She looked at Viola Taylor, who just stood there with a blank look on her face.

"Now wait a minute!" Annie interrupted. "I don't know what's going on here, and I don't care bout who did what cause I done heard enough. But I'm not gone stand here and let yall tell a bold-faced lie on *my* mama like that."

The women kept going back and forth as if Annie had never said a word.

"Woman you shut the hell up! You don't know who fathered *my* chillen." Viola snapped at Margaret, never acknowledging Annie.

"No more than you do you no-count tramp!" Margaret stepped toward Viola.

Before Annie could say another word, David stepped between the women and Ron Craw stood from where he was sitting. Lucy stood there in silence and shook her head. She couldn't believe some of the things she had just heard. The saddest part of it all she thought, was that there was a fine line between the truth and a lie in Macklin. She was known as the peace-maker, and she had to live up to her reputation and say something to end the madness that had been stirred up.

"Now ladies, I know that Dyson being killed done brought up some sadness around here, but this ain't no way to solve nothing." Lucy had gained the attention of everyone there for the moment.

Then just as she was about to speak again, Millie walked through the door. Lucy looked up once and continued talking.

"I don't think that lies are the way to solve nothing." Lucy reiterated and shook her head.

"Yeah, but the story bout your Ron and Shirley Brown sho ain't no lie now is it?" Roxy turned to Lucy. "You always did think your bread was buttered better than the rest ours, sending those boys of yours off to some college somewhere so they can be doctors, or whatever. But you listen to me Ms. Lucy," Roxy stepped closer, "You *ain't* no better than the rest of us, and your husband just as low-down as the rest of these whorish men in Macklin."

"Well at least you can use the word *was* when it comes to my Ron." Lucy stepped a little closer to Roxy. "Yeah he made a few mistakes, but the good thing is that he ain't never been crazy enough to make no more. Shame I can't say the same bout your David. You *still* tryin' to keep him from bed-hoppin, and we all know whose bed it is!"

"You just shut up!" Roxy threw her pie to the floor. "I ain't never liked your high-yellow, high and mighty behind. But I never knew just how much I hated you til right now!" Roxy lunged at Lucy and David pulled her back.

Millie didn't know what she had walked into, but she was determined to say her peace. She didn't want to disrespect Earlene, Jeb, and Ruthann, but she just couldn't hold her suspicions in any longer.

"I should have known that there ain't gone ever be no peace in this town – not even the day before Christmas, and not even after a man done been killed." Millie turned around and looked at all the faces there. Anger hung on most of them, and sadness was on the rest of them. "I know I won't make things no better by sayin' this, but I hope Linda pays for what she done to Dyson."

"That's it," Earlene screamed, "Jeb let's go right now!"

Annie ran behind them with tears in her eyes. She wondered how what was supposed to be a special gathering had turned into this all out war. Instead of bringing people closer, Dyson's death had brought out the worst in everybody.

"I wanna know what they talkin' bout you running to another man... and Dyson at that. What they talkin' bout Earlene?" Jeb was sincere.

"Not now honey. We'll talk about this at home, but right now we need to see bout Linda."

Millie continued. "I'm sorry Ms. Hicks but I have to tell this now." She looked at the floor and then back up again. "Dyson wasn't no angel by far, but he didn't deserve to be shot through the head on account of it. His daddy left him quite a bit of money, but even that money couldn't make me stay and marry a man who couldn't have no children."

"I ain't gonna stand here and listen to this." Earlene pulled at Jeb's arm.

"No wait Ms. Earlene." Millie continued. "Now a woman who sit there and have two babies by some other man while she supposed to be devoted to one, liable to do anything. And if you ask me, I think she would even kill. She would kill to be with the man she really wants – the man who the daddy to her children."

Everyone was quiet again. Then Annie broke the silence.

"Millie you come in here and accuse my only sister of killing Dyson? What kind of proof you got? You just talking crazy and everybody here knows it. Why don't you just save your stories for somebody else because my sister didn't do nothin."

"Well maybe I don't have all the proof right now but it won't be long. That leather case that Dyson was holding in his hand when they found him had things in there that will tell it all."

"How you know what was in there?" Jeb asked with his eyes squinted. "Sheriff say that they wasn't gonna release that information until they knowed more about what happened."

"Well I'm just tellin' you what the coroner told me." Millie continued. "He and my daddy are friends. There was some letters in there, the deed to that farm, and the amount of money that Dyson had in the bank. And I'm telling yall that Dyson had more money than we ever thought he had. And that ain't all." Millie turned around slowly to be sure that everyone heard her. "Dyson had those things because he wanted to sell that land and get out of town. He wanted to get as far away from Macklin and Linda as he could. You ask me, I think he found out who the daddy of Linda's babies was."

"So! That don't mean nothin! It sho don't mean Linda was the one who killed him!" Annie shouted. "My sister might be a lot of things but she ain't no stone killer!"

"Your sister, your sister." Roxy mimicked. "If only you knew what your precious sister been up to – and right up under your nose."

David snatched Roxy in his direction. It was obvious that Roxy had information that David didn't want her to share.

"Let go-a-me!" Roxy snatched her arm from David. "I'm tired of walkin' on eggshells to protect that triflin' whore."

"Roxy don't." David pleaded.

Roxy walked toward Annie. Fresh tears began forming on Roxy's face.

"Your *sister* screwed my husband! That's right, she did. And maybe all of yall knowed it. Hmph, probably talked about me good fashion behind my back too because of it. But I don't care no more. David Moss is as whorish as that hound of a daddy of his."

"That's enough Roxy!" David screamed. "You done said enough gal!"

"Go to hell David. I'm tired of being your doormat and your brother's secret keeper." Roxy stood close to Annie's face. "You ain't heard the worse honey. Linda's been screwin' your husband too. That's right... Henry and Linda been gettin' it on for years."

"You liar!" Annie spat at Roxy. "Just cause your husband can't keep his thang in his pants..."

"Now wait a minute." Annie was interrupted by Ms. Odessa. "I don't think I hardly agreed to be hostess to this mess. Yall want to argue and kill each other up then yall gonna have to take it somewhere else. Everybody get out my house!" Ms. Odessa ordered.

Surprisingly no one else said another word. Ms. Odessa had laid down the law, and no one ever heard her raise her voice in such a manner. Instead of entertaining all the talk that was going on, Ms. Odessa seemed to be the only one to remember in that moment that a man was dead, and they were there to honor his memory. She continued to speak.

"Dyson laying in the morgue and yall sittin' here going back and forth with all this who shot Dyson and callin' one another liars, whores and murderers! I can't take it, and I'm not gonna let yall disrespect Dyson nor my Zeb's memory no more!"

Everyone quietly got up and walked out of the house. They all went their separate ways and no one said goodnight to anybody. It was Christmas Eve, but the mood was far from joyous.

## 23

Jeb drove the car with fury into the night. Earlene sat beside him in silence. They never spoke a word about what was said at Ms. Odessa's house, but they both knew that it was far from over. Jeb's mind raced as he tried to piece the past together. Out of everything that had been said, he couldn't forget the accusation about Earlene and Dyson.

They pulled in front of the house and saw a light burning. Linda was probably up feeding the baby and anxious to hear another voice beside little Paul's. Jeb got out of the car and slammed the door shut as Earlene slowly followed suit. As soon as they walked in the door, Linda was sitting in the front room nursing Paul.

"How was the service this evening?" She whispered so she wouldn't startle Paul, who had fallen asleep with his mouth still at her breast.

When neither one of them answered her, she sensed that something had happened.

"Is anybody got they ears on? I don't wanna shout and wake the baby."

Earlene finally answered, "It was fine baby. Reverend Poe did a fine job like always."

Jeb walked straight into the bedroom and never said a word.

"What's wrong with daddy?" Linda finally asked as she gently pulled the baby away from her chest.

"Don't worry bout your daddy. He just a little upset is all… he'll be alright. I'm going in there after him. You need anythang before I turn in?"

"No ma'am." Linda smiled, still trying to get used to Earlene treating her so kind. "I'm gone put this boy down then have me some cake. I'll see yall in the morning."

Earlene walked away from Linda through the kitchen and into the bedroom. Jeb was sitting on the bed with his back to her. She walked over to where he was and looked at his face. He was sitting there with tears in his eyes and a bottle of moonshine in his hand. Earlene couldn't understand what she was seeing because Jeb hadn't drank in years. Something about him had changed in a matter of moments. She wasn't sure what it was and then he spoke.

"You know, one of the hardest thangs I ever done in my life was to put down this bottle. I took my first drank when I was a boy sittin' on the porch with my granddaddy. You know he always said that a lil drank every now and again keep a man good and strong."

"Honey, I…"

Jeb interrupted Earlene's response. "But I guess I never learned jest how to have a lil drank at all. I guess some folks can't handle the temptation of having a lil of nothin. When I married you though, seem like I knowed that I would be alright. You was the prettiest thang I seed in all my days. I knowed Ms. Ruthann didn't hardly want you to marry me, but I was bent on tryin' to prove myself. When times got hard and I got afraid of how I would keep my family from missing a meal, I turned to this here." He lifted the bottle into the air.

Jeb looked right at Earlene and said with fury, "You and them gals was the reason I worried myself so and picked up a drank more than I should have. And you and them gals was the reason I put it down and swore to never pick it up again. I kept this last bottle right in that trunk over yonder." Jeb pointed to the corner with the bottle. "Put it in there the day I swore to never touch it again." He paused for a moment. "I never took it out till right now."

Earlene now had tears in her eyes. "Baby I know you thinkin' bout what Roxy said tonight bout me and Dyson. I just want to…"

"Don't you waste your breath on nary explanation woman. Just tell me if it's true!" Jeb yelled at Earlene.

Earlene stood there, her feet glued to her spot. She hadn't seen Jeb this enraged since he was drinking. Although she was afraid and confused, she finally answered in a timid voice.

"Yes."

Jeb stood abruptly from the bed and slammed the bottle against the dresser. Glass sprayed across the floor, and the moonshine splashed on their legs. The liquor shined in the darkness, making it look like they had just jumped into the shallow end of a river.

"Damn you to hell woman!" Before he knew what was happening, Jeb had grabbed Earlene by her neck. His grip was closing in on her, and she tussled with him for a moment and managed to snatch away.

"Jeb Hicks! I know you mad, but God in Heaven know I don't deserve this, not after everythang I done put up with from you!"

"The hell you say." Jeb failed to regain his composure and backed away from Earlene. "I know I ain't always done right by you, but woman this here is somethin' else altogether, so don't you fix your mouth to mention God to me." Jeb's faced twisted in amazement, and his voice was between a whisper and a scream. He grabbed his stomach as if he was in pain, as he questioned Earlene with just one word. "Dyson?"

Earlene pleaded as if her life depended on it.

"Jeb baby, it was a long time ago. And it was when you was doing all that drinking and carryin' on. I would be out of my mind sometimes, afraid for me and afraid for those gals. I ain't sayin' it was right, but you got to listen to me and let me tell you how it was."

"Listen to you?" Jeb asked blankly.

"Honey please?"

Jeb sat back down on the bed trying to understand how in the course of a day he'd gone from being grateful for everything he had to wishing he was dead. Hurt entered his body and danced on his insides. The smell of the liquor had overtaken the room and slowly began to choke him.

He tried to control it, but his insides couldn't hold hurt and the smell of liquor at the same time. He vomited violently on the side of the bed. He doubled over holding his stomach as he fell to his knees. Everything that had tormented him all his life seemed to cover the bedroom floor. Earlene stood there shaking and crying, not having the slightest idea how to help her husband.

Linda heard a shatter from her parents' room, then quickly glanced down at Paul. He hadn't budged. Even if she was unclear about what happened while they were out, Linda was sure that her parents were having it out now about whatever it was. She crept to their bedroom door and listened. She heard sobs from Earlene but nothing else. She jerked back quickly and sniffed the air. She smelled liquor.  Suddenly she was taken back in her mind to the days when Jeb was drinking.  All she could do was wonder, just what would cause her father to drink again after all these years?

*     *     *

David and Roxy rode in silence as they headed back to their farm.  Roxy stared blankly into the darkness and thought about everything that had been said.  She finally broke the silence with a voice that was raspy from yelling.

"So how long you gonna hurt me before you figure it's enough?"

David continued to drive in silence.

"You know David, I thought I could live with your ways long enough till you got good and tired of them."  Fresh tears welled in Roxy's eyes.  "But I realize that maybe what everybody say bout you, your brothers, and your daddy is true.  Maybe yall Moss men ain't got it in you to be true to one woman."

David slowly pulled the car into the drive going toward their house.  They had left the children at home this year because their youngest, David Jr., was sick with a fever.  They had four children and had been married for thirteen years.  The oldest was a girl they named Hannah, who had been seeing after her younger siblings since she was eight years old.  She saw to it that they were fed, bathed, and clothed every day.  She was becoming a young woman herself, and Roxy couldn't bear to face it.  The children had been all she held on to for most of her marriage.

There weren't any lights on in the house; Hannah had put the little ones to bed.  David and Roxy sat in silence once more as they looked at the house. Just as David touched the handle to open the door, Roxy grabbed his arm.

"Ain't you got nothin' to say? You done had a chile by another woman, and ain't you got nothin' to say?"

"What you talkin' bout now woman? You think I'm the one knocked Linda up?" David's anger finally got the best of him. "Well them ain't none of my chillun!"

"I'm not talkin' bout Linda and you know it. Lawd knows she ain't lil miss innocent either, but that ain't who I'm talkin' bout now." Roxy's voice bellowed through the car, the raspiness in her throat less obvious.

"Then who the hell you talkin' bout?"

"Viola Taylor!" Roxy shouted. "That last baby of hers is the image of you." Roxy wiped at the tears on her face with the back of her hand. "I know all about it David. You hangin' in Blake's til all hours then goin' over to Viola's place. She don't live two spits from Reverend Poe, and God and everybody in this town know how much that wife of his talk." Roxy became silent for a moment, then shook her head. "I done taken all I'm gonna take off o' you."

David looked in his wife's eyes in the darkness, her tears still glistening on her face. "So what you sayin' Roxy?"

"I'm leaving you David."

"Leavin' me hell!" David shouted. "Where you think you gonna go?"

Roxy let out a boisterous chuckle with tears still in her eyes and irony in her voice. "I don't even care. Just as long as I get as far away from you and this town as my legs will take me."

"You a fool woman if you think you can make it without me." David said with a smug look on his face.

"Maybe I am. I may even be the biggest dang fool God ever made, but I won't be *your* fool no more." Roxy opened the car door and slammed it so hard her fingers tingled.

*     *     *

Sassy Flo rocked to the music in Blake's tavern, sipping on a hot toddy that Blake had made just for her. She was a regular at his place, so he always gave her a little extra something.

The rumor mill in town had long since linked Sassy Flo and Blake together, despite her outward flirting with other men. People in town said that Blake's wife had put the scar on Sassy Flo's forehead with a butcher knife one night, after she'd caught them in the corner of the saloon after closing. There was never any real proof that the incident ever happened, but in Macklin, proof was the last thing that was needed for a juicy story to stand.

The waitress walked over to Sassy Flo and offered her assistance.

"Can I get you another sugar?"

Sassy Flo focused on the waitress's face as she continued in her state of nostalgia. "Why don't you go on home? It's Christmas Eve don't you know. I'm sho you gat somebody waitin' at home for you." Sassy Flo turned from her and continued swaying.

The waitress shook her head and walked away. She walked to the bar where Blake was standing.

"Think I'll head on out boss. The place is empty anyhow ceptin' your friend over yonder." She threw her head in Sassy Flo's direction.

"Ok, I'll close up." Blake stretched his arms out and yawned. "Merry Christmas! Be careful out there now cause folks in this town done stooped to killin."

"I'll be fine. Hank out front waitin' on me. Yall have a good night and a merry Christmas." The waitress removed her apron and headed toward the front door.

Blake walked toward Sassy Flo, who was the only person in the place. He pulled her close to him and kissed her on the mouth. She continued to sway to the music that was still playing. Blake pulled back and looked her in the eyes.

Sassy Flo moved her full hips from side to side before resting them close to Blake. When she spoke, her words seemed to seep into Blake's skin. Her scent drove him wild.

"You promised me that you would, and I been patient enough. Now tell me what you know bout Dyson."

Blake never could resist Sassy Flo, even after his wife found out about them. He surrendered and told her everything that Dyson told him the day before he was killed.

# 24

Annie tossed in the night like an uncontrolled ship. Her dreams started off normal as always, but she soon drifted into the nightmares that she had grown accustomed to. She saw Dyson dressed in white and waiving a red flag. Linda was holding her new baby boy, but the baby had a grown man's face. Annie looked a little closer, and the face bore a stark resemblance to her own son Isaiah, but the features were more prominent. The baby's eyes were as black as a crow's coat, and his mouth was smiling, showing a full row of pearly white teeth.

Annie trembled at the sight of the baby and screamed until she thought her throat would go numb, but not a sound came out. She began to run into the darkness to escape the images before her, but her legs wouldn't move as fast as she wanted them to. She felt as if her legs were weighed down by logs, and her body weakened before giving in completely. She collapsed into a pool of some thick sticky substance that she discovered was blood. She looked all around her and belted out another soundless scream. An arm arose out of the scarlet pool and clawed at her face. She submitted to the force and fell lifeless as her body convulsed.

"Annie! Annie!" Henry shook her and watched sweat poor from her face as she struggled with yet another bad dream. "Baby wake up – you just dreamin' again."

Annie finally stopped to focus on what was reality. Henry was holding on to her arm and fanning her face.

"What time is it? What, what day this is? Henry?" Her words stumbled out of her mouth into the dark room where all she could see was the outline of Henry's face.

"You had another dream baby. It's Christmas day, but not quite, it be bout 3'o'clock in the morning. You come in last night from Ms. Odessa's all in a fuss bout Linda being accused of killing Dyson and some big ruckus over there."

"What else did I say?" Annie interrupted Henry.

"Nothin' cept you was real tired and wanted to get to bed. I looked in on the chillen one more time and made sho you got to sleep alright yourself. Guess I fell asleep not long after you did. What happened over there last night? You was in a huff like I ain't never seen before." Henry rubbed Annie's back.

Annie closed her eyes for a moment and remembered that she had decided not to confront Henry about Roxy's accusations about him and Linda, not yet anyway. She had promised herself that she was going to try to get through Dyson's murder and all of the hellish goings on without destroying herself or her family. She only wanted to sleep and forget about the seam in Macklin that was becoming a tear. She had decided last night to forget that she'd heard that Earlene had slept with Dyson, and that old Zeb had fathered two of Viola Taylor's children.

She wanted to at least pretend that Linda was as good a person as she had wanted her to be her whole life. Yes, she had decided to ignore all the bitterness she felt in her belly as Earlene and Jeb dropped her off after they left Ms. Odessa's house. She would even pretend that silence and rage hadn't engulfed the three of them as they drove into the night. She had drifted into a restless sleep battling her emotions, and now she was face to face with them as

Henry held her arm and rubbed her back. It was Christmas day, but Annie felt empty. She lay back on the bed and breathed slowly, thinking of a way to ask her husband if he had been sleeping with her sister.

*     *     *

Eddie was restless as he lay in his bed. Although his body yearned for it, sleep escaped him. He couldn't shake the sick feeling in his stomach as he thought about Linda being pregnant with another man's child. His anger had gotten the best of him, and he had wanted to get as far away from Macklin, Mississippi as possible. He had fooled himself into thinking that he could be happy with Linda and come to her hometown and rescue her like they did in the movies. He didn't have a lot of money, but his gigs at the hottest night spots in Chicago kept his pockets close to full.

He had envisioned Linda's smile and her sweet scent all the nights he played in those clubs. Every woman he saw didn't compare to Linda in his mind. He was so obsessed with her that he had failed to tell her that he was already married. He pondered for years over how he could make it up to her somehow and felt that he had lost her forever, until she wrote him a letter.

Now he was back in Chicago in his bed, the winter air whistling outside his second floor window. Snow completely covered the ground, and there was a pale green glare that shined outside in the darkness. It was the middle of the night, Christmas Eve night, and all he could think about was Linda.

The woman lying in bed next to him snored as Eddie's thoughts went back to Macklin just two days before. Eddie had made himself believe that Linda was being hurt and manipulated by the man she was pregnant by. When that waitress gave him the directions to Dyson McCloud's farm, he had every intention of heading straight over there to put the man in his place.

Eddie huffed as he remembered standing behind a tree watching this man. He had asked himself what he would gain by confronting someone who probably didn't know him from Nat Turner. So, instead of marching over to this Dyson McCloud, who appeared to be busy anyway, he had decided to do what he thought was best. Before he changed his mind, Eddie had ducked from behind the tree, turned around, and ran as fast as he could. He had headed back to Macklin station and waited for the eight o'clock train.

While he had waited in the station, he told himself that he must forget about Linda Hicks; that she was just someone who had come into his life when he really needed someone, but he would now have to let her go. When the train for Chicago had pulled up, he was about as anxious to get on as a chicken was going to the chopping block. He was sure that once he boarded the train that Linda would be a distant memory. He had felt that he would never have her now that she had two children by another man. She belonged to the man he had seen, and it was time for him to let her go.

As Eddie lay there in his bed, his eyes finally fell heavy and gave in to sleep. It was the wind outside that soothed his heart and not the silhouette that lie in bed next to him. He had only just met the woman hours before and wasn't even sure of her name. But to Eddie, something as insignificant as her name didn't matter to him at all, especially because her name wasn't Linda Hicks.

## 25

The morning sun rose on Macklin like it did every Christmas. A light frost covered the ground, and the sky beamed with billowy clouds and pale blue sketches. Smoke rose from the chimneys of the tiny homes, and even the farm animals seemed to be in a rested state.

Linda awakened to quietness. The aroma of sweet potato pie and ham filled the house. Baby Paul flinched as she shifted her weight in bed. She didn't have to wonder from the wonderful smells if Earlene and Ruthann were awake yet, as they always were up before the sun on an early Christmas morning. Every time Linda attempted to feel glad, guilt forced the feeling back down her throat and into the pit of her stomach. She lay her head back down on her pillow. Her thoughts turned over in her mind as she finally accepted that Dyson was really dead and that she might be responsible.

Earlene hadn't slept the night before. After Jeb got sick and threw up in the bedroom, he had lay back on the bed for a while before getting up and leaving the house. Earlene didn't have the strength or the courage to ask him where he was going that time of night. She cleaned up the evidence of hurt that came from Jeb's stomach and sat down in the rocking chair next to the window in the bedroom.

As the sun rose, she could hear Ruthann humming from the next room, intensely aware of what had gone on. Ruthann was never left in the dark about anything, and Earlene was certain that this time would hold no exceptions. She washed her face in the basin that sat on the dresser and dried it slowly. She had never thought that the day would come when Jeb found out about her and Dyson. The affair happened during a time in which neither one of them cared to remember. All the fussing Earlene had done about Dyson and Linda was for her own contentment, as well as Linda's own good. She didn't want her daughter to be with a man that she had been with. She could never tell Linda that she wouldn't stand for something like that, so she just kept her secret to herself. She had faced her husband, now she had to face her grandmother, and an even more daunting thought, her children. She finally gathered her nerve and headed to the kitchen.

*    *    *

Millie helped her mother prepare her customary Christmas breakfast: Fried ham that had been cured, scrambled eggs, homemade biscuits, and Ms. Erma's famous strawberry preserves. Everybody in the house was up and ready to eat except Millie, who had a lump in her throat. She remembered that Dyson would go to Cobb County every year and buy apples and oranges for everybody. Although she has loved her husband of six years, she always kept a place in heart for Dyson.

"You alright dawta?" Mrs. Henderson asked Millie.

"Yes ma'am, I'll be alright." Millie feigned a smile. "I was just thinking that's all. Yall better tell papa to come on in here 'fo all the preserves is gone."

Mr. Henderson walked into the kitchen and kissed his wife. They could tell he was feeling better because he shouted the same words he did before every one of his meals.

"Ah'm so hungry I could eat the side of a mule!"

"Daddy that ain't funny now and it ain't never been funny." Millie shook her head.

"Yall shush up now and let's eat." Mr. Henderson mumbled as he plopped down in a chair.

They all sat down to the table and tried to enjoy their traditional Christmas breakfast. Despite the blissful occasion, they ate in silence. The forks clanked against the plates in a uniformed rhythm. With the exception of one of Mr. Henderson's grunts from savoring his food, the air was still. As they continued their meal, there was banging at the door. Millie stood up and walked through the kitchen and into the front room. The banging seemed to increase as she made her way closer to the door. She finally snatched it open with urgency.

"Girl, I thought I was gonna have to knock this door down!" Cassie pushed her way inside. "I know *everybody* in here ain't gone deaf."

"We was sittin' down tryin' to enjoy our Christmas breakfast, and I guess we was crazy enough to think everybody else round here was at home doin the same." Millie responded with less enthusiasm than she had expected.

Cassie panted, "Well Merry Christmas and all that, but I got somethin' to tell you bout.."

"Linda?" Millie interrupted before Cassie could finish. "I knew it! She might be able to fool them simple-minded folks of hers, but she can't fool me one bit!"

"Chile, would you get your mind off Linda? My news ain't about her. It's about Dyson." Cassie put her hands on her hips.

The excitement in Millie's eyes faded, and the accusatory look disappeared from her face. "What about Dyson? Can't be nothin', except maybe that they done finally found out just *how* Linda pulled that trigger on that shotgun; hell, they already know *why* she did it."

"Millie, who done come here on Christmas mornin'?" Mrs. Henderson bellowed from the kitchen.

"It ain't nobody but Cassie mama, and she *ain't stayin'*." Millie put emphasis on the last two words as she answered her mother and looked directly at Cassie.

"I ain't goin' nowhere, least not til' I tell you what Sassy Flo told me last night." Cassie's words had lowered to a whisper. "Now you need to listen to me and listen to me good. Sassy Flo say that Blake told her that Dyson had plans to leave Macklin. Blake say Dyson come into his place the day before they found Dyson dead and told him that he couldn't stay in town. Dyson said that he knowed bout Linda and the man who really fathered them babies and that he was gonna tell Linda that she could have him.

"Dyson had went and took all his money out the bank over in Cobb County and was gonna sell his place. Chile, Dyson had enough money to buy this whole town if he wanted to! Anyway, Blake say that the onliest person who knowed bout Dyson leavin' was Henry Moss. That ain't all chile – Dyson told Blake that he believed that Henry was the father of Linda's children. Said he knowed that the two of them had been messin' around for some years and that Linda didn't know that he couldn't give her no babies."

Cassie went on without so much as taking a breath. Millie finally intervened with a look on her face that was a cross between anger and bewilderment.

"Gal, I thought you had some news. All you done just said, I could have told you bout it better than you just told me. Don't you know I'm the one who told everybody this same thang over to Ms. Odessa's house last night? And you say Blake told Sassy Flo all of this last night too?"

"As sho as I'm standin' here." Cassie finally breathed.

Millie walked over to the window and looked out at nothing in particular. It was starting to make sense to her now. If Henry was the father of Linda's children, then surely Henry must have had a hand in killing Dyson. Millie thought that even if Linda didn't pull the trigger after all, she had still committed an inconceivable crime. Linda had slept with her own sister's husband. As if Cassie could read her thoughts, Millie looked at her friend and decided that something had to be done.

Cassie broke the silence. "What you think we oughta do?"

Fresh tears made their way to the corners of Millie's eyes. "We gonna let the Lord take of it."

"The Lord?" Cassie's voice finally went up a few octaves. "What happened to all that fire in your belly bout how Linda should pay if she was responsible for killin' Dyson? Ain't she still guilty?"

"I guess the Lord will take of her too. She the one got to live with what's done happened. I'm sure the guilt from that alone is whippin' her right good bout now."

\*     \*     \*

David Moss awakened to a quiet house. For the first time in years, there was no breakfast cooking on the stove, no children singing, and no Roxy there to kiss his lips and wish him a Merry Christmas. She had left him just as she'd promised. When they had arrived home the night before, Roxy had awakened the children and packed up three trunks before David realized she had actually been serious about leaving him. He hadn't put up a fight, which surprised him. He had watched her as she pulled clothes from the drawers and wrapped dishes carefully in crape paper.

There were no words exchanged between the two of them, and Roxy had even sentenced the children to silence and forbad them to ask any questions. David just watched helplessly as he sat on the bed they had shared for thirteen years. Before her and the kids walked out of the door just before day that morning, Roxy had told him that she would be staying with her parents for a while in Jackson.

It was Christmas morning, and David's life had taken a turn that he had never expected. Roxy had put up with his gambling, his infidelity, and his rotten attitude toward her and the children from time to time.

He knew that he couldn't rely on his father because he had burned that bridge a long time before. His father had stopped giving him money when he realized that his son had gambling problems. With Roxy and the children gone, he thought that a fresh start would be just what he needed, especially since it wouldn't be long before the rest of his world would begin to crumble. He, too, would leave Macklin for good.

David suddenly thought about the war and all the friends he had lost. The grisly images of tattered limbs and bloody heads now danced before him. During the war he had convinced himself that if he could just make it back home to safety, he would appreciate life that much more. Now as he sat in an empty house with a bottle of gin in his hand, he wondered if making it back to Macklin was indeed a blessing, or if he wouldn't have been better off numbered among the dead in the south of France.

\*       \*       \*

Annie awakened to voices of the children laughing and whispering. She lay there a moment and pictured Hester and Isaiah's faces all lit up with the expectation of Christmas candy and presents. Annie's heart prepared to rejoice – then she remembered. Henry's deep voice slid between the children's high pitched excitement. Bitterness formed at the corners of Annie's mouth, and she couldn't help but frown as the taste of bile made its way from her stomach to the back of her throat.

She quickly grabbed the bucket she kept by the side of the bed and heaved over it. She wondered if it was the morning sickness that turned her stomach or the sound of Henry's voice. She sat up in the bed and listened closer to the voices on the other side of the door. Henry had gotten up before she did and awakened the children. She rubbed her belly and cringed at the thought of carrying another child for him. She couldn't understand what she was feeling. She knew that she loved Henry with all she had, but she wondered how he could love her *and* do what he did.

Before she had time to search her thoughts for answers, Henry snatched the bedroom door open. The children came running into the room yelling, "Merry Christmas mama!" Annie feigned a smile and hugged Hester, Emma, and Isaiah. Annie locked her eyes on Emma's little face and held her gaze. Emma looked exactly like Linda, but for the first time, she wondered who else her little niece might resemble. Sarah climbed into Annie's lap and wrapped her tiny arms around Annie's neck, practically choking her in the process. Henry stood back – a spectator of a moment that he didn't feel worthy enough to be a part of.

"Merry Christmas!" Annie managed the words with phlegm still in her throat.

"Mama, we going to grandma and grandpa's house?" Hester pleaded.

"Maybe after breakfast."

"Yay!" The children yelled in unison.

Henry walked toward the bed, "Come on now and let mama get herself together."

As he started to walk out with the children, Annie called after him. "Henry, I…"

As if he was one with her thoughts, Henry let the children out of the room and closed the door.

Silence and tension waltzed around the room with fearlessness. The two of them quickly became on guard. Before Henry could even utter a word, Annie's fury finally showed up.

"There ain't nothin' you can say to me Henry, so save your breath. You think because it's Christmas I'm supposed to act like I don't know what I know?" She made her way out of the bed and yanked at her housecoat that hung on the bed post.

"Baby, I…"

"Don't you dare *baby* me Henry. Speakin' of babies – I hate that I'm carryin' another one for you after what you done."

Henry grabbed for Annie's arm. "Baby that just ain't fair. Why would you go and say somethin' like that?"

"Fair?" Annie mimicked. "And screwin' my only sister is fair Henry? Don't fix your mouth to me about what's fair and what ain't. I done give you all of me, till I can't give no more. I done loved you for nearly eight years and ain't never looked at another man, much less touched one. I done stood up for you against my own mama and my great-granny. I done had three babies for you and carryin' another right now. I done cooked, cleaned, and washed your drawls – I done taken better care of you than your own mama did, and what thanks have I got? Nothin' – except you givin' it to my sister behind my back."

Henry stood there squeezing the response that threatened to come from his lips inside of his mouth. He wanted to carefully choose his words to make sure that whatever he said didn't feed the fire to Annie's rant. *What could he say?* He thought to himself. *What words in the English language could possibly defend or justify a man's sleeping with his wife's sister?* He gave up on trying to find the right thing to say and just stood there.

Annie didn't let up. "So you gonna just stand there and not even give me no kind of answer? I ain't worth that much to you?"

Henry remained silent. He couldn't help but to think about how confusing Annie's requests were. First, she ordered him to silence and dared him to speak, and now she was impatiently awaiting his response.

"Answer me!" Annie's thunderous voice seemed to shake the room.

Henry looked at her with bewilderment– his lips still sealed with guilt; his eyes heavy with shame.

"I don't know what to say to make it better Annie, so I hope you pardon me for not saying nothin' at all."

The water in Annie's eyes finally tumbled down her cheeks. She eased back down on the bed, hoping that the vomit would obey her will and not come up again. As much as she wanted to unleash the anger within her, Annie held on to the little dignity she felt she had left. She wanted to do more than kill Henry – that wouldn't be justice. She wanted him to feel the hurt that she was suffering at that very moment.

As Henry stood there wrapped in stillness, Annie suddenly remembered that he was not alone in his crime. Her tears flowed more freely as she thought about his accomplice in the matter. She thought about Linda and the baby that could very well be her husband's

.

\*     \*     \*

Jeb awakened in a bed that wasn't his. He remembered how close he came to sipping the moonshine the night before and how he could no longer stand the smell of liquor, let alone the taste. He had left Earlene in tears for the first time in years, only this time, they were tears of shame on her part instead of tears of hurt from one of his many tirades. As he slowly gathered himself and lifted his head from the pillow, he heard the faint voices of Reverend Poe and his wife from the next room.

Reverend Poe had always told his church members that if they needed him day or night, he would be there. Jeb didn't hesitate in holding the reverend to that promise the night before. As Jeb collected his thoughts, he attempted to piece together the chain of events that led him to where he was. He retraced the years of his marriage, outlining every disagreement that he could think of between him and Earlene.  He had doubted many things in the world, down to the very existence of God, but never had he doubted that his wife would remain faithful to him.

Somehow the world looked different to him as he peered around the tiny spare room.  There was an old chest that sat in the corner, a tiny oil lamp on a table, and the very bed he was sitting on.  The room smelled of pine and camphor, but he didn't worry himself as to why.  Jeb's only concern at the moment was getting through the next day and the day after that.  He wondered how the town that he had known all of his life had suddenly turned into a place he didn't recognize at all.  Dyson was dead, Earlene was a cheat, and he was contemplating leaving Macklin for good.

"Don't you think we oughta go in there and make sho he doin' alright?"  Mrs. Poe attempted to whisper to her husband as they sat at breakfast.  "I mean, the man came here in the middle of the night wrecked with trouble.  Least we can do is to make sho he ain't done nothin' crazy in there."

"Woman, calm yourself.  That man' alright, he probably just tired is all.  Ain't every day somebody like Jeb Hicks come knockin' on the door that time of mownin' with tears runnin' down his face.  Ah reckon we oughta just let him rest a while 'fore we go in there meddlin with him."  Reverend Poe took a bite of his biscuit.

"Well how we know that he ain't the one that kilt Dyson and that his guilt done finally got to him?  I done heard folks whisperin' bout that wife of his and Dyson for years now.  I ain't feedin' no murderer – and on Christmas day at that!"  Mrs. Poe poured more coffee and set the pot down with a jolt with her last word.

"Cause ah done knowed Jeb too many years to be-lieve he can do a thang like that, Alice.  Now when he good and ready to come outta that room and bother us bout what's done happened at home, that's when he'll do it.  Till then, let's just enjoy our breakfast.  Ah got enough to thank about with Dyson's funeral being planned for two days from today."

Since Dyson didn't have any family left in Macklin, Reverend Poe had taken the liberty of planning Dyson's funeral.  The task was supposed to be Linda's, but Rever-end Poe and his wife had gladly accepted when Earlene asked.  Earlene had decided that Annie and Henry were in no shape to plan either.  Reverend Poe had been good friends with Dyson's father before he passed away, and the reverend had treated Dyson like a son ever since.  He was known for treating every man in town with the uttermost respect.

The couple continued their meal while listening for the door of the spare room to open.  It never did.

# 26

"I ain't never seent nothin' like this long as I been sheriff of this town." Sheriff Mann shook his head as the coroner finished the story about the three shotgun holes left in Dyson's body. Sheriff Mann was tall and thin with a deep olive complexion. He was a white man with questionable features – at least that's how the people in Macklin had always described him. *Just like Abraham Lincoln*, they had often whispered.

"I mean, you think you know people and then something like this up and happens. Guess you can't put nothin' pass nobody these days." He shifted his weight from one foot to the other.

The coroner finished shuffling some papers, not really giving his full attention to Sheriff Mann. He had complained the whole morning long about working on Christmas day. He pulled a can from the side of his desk and spit a mouth full of brown liquid in it. He then looked up as if the sheriff had just entered the room.

"Well, three shotgun holes be a pretty sight compared to some of what I done seen. Folks ate up from the inside out after lying dead in a house for days in heat that the devil himself wouldn't sit up in. Yeah, I done seen some things. But I must admit, I didn't take ole Dyson here for the trouble makin' kind. I mean sho, he had a few enemies, but you show me a man on earth who don't." Sweat formed in beads on the coroner's forehead, even though the tiny room was drafty and dank.

Sheriff Mann pulled a brown leather case from his back pocket. He cleared his throat, still unable to stand the stale smell of formaldehyde. The coroner's office was adjacent to the morgue, and the scent wafted through the walls effortlessly. He pulled a handkerchief from his other pocket and coughed into it. When he got a free breath, he spoke.

"I reckon this will be all we need to start questionin' that Hicks gal. Dyson left a note here telling her that he knew that those chillen wasn't his. He explains how he loved her, but he couldn't stick around to be shamed no more than he already had been. He left her a little bit of cash, but he was intended to sell that house and all that land of his. There's also a train ticket and a bankbook that shows that he had $33,000 put away. I reckon she just couldn't let all that money walk away from her. You ask me, I think it says it all right here."

"Well that's a fine interpretation sheriff, but sounds like you pretty darn sure of what done taken place." The coroner took the leather case from Sheriff Mann and examined it. "Question right now is - who gets all this loot now?"

"Well, Reverend Poe the closest thing to any kind of father to him, but I reckon we can't say just now."

The coroner handed the case back to Sheriff Mann. "I only hope it's as simple as all this. Cause iffen it ain't, seems we got ourselves a manhunt."

"Don't we just."

*     *     *

Annie tried her best to give the children a decent Christmas. She wanted to spend the entire day in bed feeling sorry for herself, but Ruthann had always told her, *Once you have chillen, your life stop being your own.* Annie had been sure of that from the day that Hester was born.

She had forced herself from the bedroom to make breakfast. Then the children opened their presents which were fruit, new shoes, and candy. Annie was glad that they were happy with what they had gotten. Between her family and Henry's, they were blessed compared to a lot of the children in Macklin. The day went on and dinner had been served.

As Annie swallowed the cured ham, she also swallowed the hurt that threatened to suffocate her. As she digested the cornbread dressing, she searched for a way to do the same with the pain of confronting Linda about her and Henry. As she savored the pecan pie, she savored the days of peace when Linda was still in Chicago, living the life of her dreams, and far away from Macklin. Now, all Annie wanted for was Christmas was for Linda to have never come back to Macklin.

*     *     *

Ruthann tried to uplift Earlene's spirits by telling her to hold her new grandson. As much as she wanted to enjoy Christmas though, Earlene's mind was riddled with guilt over the fight that she and Jeb had, as well as worry over where he had gone.

Linda hadn't left the house since Paul had been born. She had told Ruthann and Earlene that she wanted to make sure Dyson had a decent funeral. They assured her that Reverend Poe was taking care of everything. Linda knew that she would eventually have to face the dreadful moment of telling them everything, so as she helped her mother and grandmother prepare dinner, she finally broke. She sat down in a chair in the kitchen with tears in her eyes.

"Mama, grandma, I did something terrible."

Earlene dried her hands on her apron and walked over to Linda. She secretly asked God to give her enough strength to comfort her daughter because she was still heartbroken herself over her and Jeb. Linda asked where Jeb was earlier that morning. When Earlene just looked at her and shook her head, she knew that she had lived long enough to know to just drop it. Linda knew that her parents had had a falling out the night before and that Jeb had probably gone somewhere to clear his head.

"What is it baby?" Earlene rubbed Linda's head. In that moment she tried to understand the depth of love she had for her daughter. She had spent so many years bonding with Annie and not Linda, that it now felt strange.

"Mama I…"

As Linda was speaking, Annie, Henry and the children walked through the door. Linda's words stopped, and her tears flowed more freely.

As if everyone knew what was about to take place, the atmosphere in the kitchen changed. There were no exchanges of Merry Christmas and no hugs to go around. With the children in the front room with Ruthann, Annie immediately started in on Linda.

"I guess you gone cry your way through this too Linny? How could you do this me?" The anger in Annie's voice was apparent, and Henry attempted to grab her before it had gotten the best of her.

"Do what?" Earlene asked out of concern, but more so out of confusion.

"Screw Henry, that's what!"

"What? What is going on here? Henry is this true?" Earlene demanded.

"Ms. Earlene this ain't the time or the place." Henry then turned to Annie while still having her arm tight within his grip. "Annie you promised me that you wouldn't say nothin' bout this today. You promised that you would wait until everything with the funeral and the holidays was over to even mention it."

"Well I lied!" Annie spat the words out like venom. "Am I a bad person now because I can't hold my tongue about the two of you sneaking around behind my back for Lord only knows how long?"

Linda finally conjured up enough nerve to respond to Annie's accusations.

"Annie, I didn't mean to hurt you. It just… I don't know why, but it just happened."

Ruthann had put the children in Earlene's bedroom and walked into the kitchen where everyone was by then. Her presence alone shifted the atmosphere once again. Before she could catch herself, Earlene had rushed toward Henry and slapped him across the face. He didn't flinch.

Annie broke away from Henry and marched toward Linda. Linda stood abruptly, afraid of Annie's next move.

"Just happened?" Annie's fury was now full-fledged, and no one dared stand in her way. "Linny, you done had bout every man in this town. Did you just *have* to have my husband too? Would it have killed you to think about me and my children? I can't believe that I stood up for you against people all these years when all along they was right. You ain't nothin' more than a common whore. And I didn't know Shirley Brown for myself, but I would stake all the money I got and my children's lives on the fact that you ain't no better than she was."

"Annie, you don't mean that." Linda said through trembling lips.

"I mean it Linny, and I ain't got nothin' more to say to you ever. Don't ever come near my husband or my children again!"

"Now wait a minute missy. You come in here yellin' and carryin' on at your sister, and your husband is just as guilty as he wanna be in this thing!" Earlene had told Henry to leave the kitchen after she had slapped him. "I tried to tell you 'fore you even married this boy that he wasn't no good just like his daddy and brothers, but you was bent on provin' me wrong I guess. Now look what he done did – done caused this mess between you and your sister with his ole doggish ways."

Ruthann finally spoke up after listening to the bickering.

"Ah always told yall that Heaven was watching and sees all thangs." Ruthann's voice was strong and deep. "Because of wrong choices that all of you done made, this is the saddest Christmas that ah done seed since 'mancipation. Earlene, don't be on that gal 'cause she wants to stand by huh husband. Lawd knows you done stood by yourn when ah didn't thank you should have. This here thang is between Annie and Linda. Ah don't wanna see them at each other's throats no more than you do, but what's done is done. You ain't been no angel your own self, and your husband runnin' out of here last night done proved just that."

Silence crept in again. No one said anything for a few minutes after Ruthann finished talking. Over the years it had become an unspoken rule. When she made a speech, her words brought something over everyone within earshot, commanding them to silence. Annie broke the silence.

"All hell done broke loose in this family, and ain't nobody willing to take the responsibility for it. Dyson's funeral is in two days, and I don't even know if I have the strength to even go." Her voice cracked as she spoke, not looking at anyone in particular.

Her gaze was fixed on the kitchen floor. The speckles in the wood seemed to swirl into a pattern, hypnotizing her. "I don't know what to do." She burst into tears. Linda came over to Annie and held her. Annie didn't resist; she just folded into her embrace.

The next few days in Macklin were quiet. Everyone in town stayed in and ate the Christmas dinners that they barely touched on the day itself. The weather was indecisive.

Jeb had been comforted by Reverend Poe and his wife the last couple of days, but he missed his family. It was the first Christmas he had ever spent away from them since he had been married. He knew that he had to come to his senses and go home eventually, but he just had to figure out how. Reverend Poe had asked him the night before if he was ready to talk about it. Even though Jeb wasn't ready to do so, he obliged the man who had taken him in during the wee hours of the morning.

"I don't know reverend. I just never figured Earlene for the two-timin' kind. I guess a man's drinkin' is liable to cause a woman to do 'bout anything."

"Don't ah know it. Reverend Poe cleared his throat. "My own daddy was a dranker. Took my mama and us chillen through plum hell 'fore he died. Ah guess ah made a vow to the Lawd way back then to never have no parts of liquor – not if that's what it did to folks. I reckon Earlene was just hurtin' during that time, and Dyson's arms was the onliest comfort she could find." He went on.

"Some folks say that the fastest way to drive a woman to another man's arms is to stop showin' her that attention you gave huh when you first tried to win huh heart. Now ah believe in the Word of God, but it ain't never hurt to listen to common sense neither. Womens is just like babies – they never stop wantin' to be held, and they will cry and cry 'til you pick 'em up and put 'em back on your lap.

"Ah know you hurtin' Jeb. Believe you me, ah wouldn't want to be in your shoes, but sometimes the Lawd will take us to our knees and let us feel some of the pain that we done 'flicted on others. Ah ain't sayin' that God ain't forgiven you for what you done when you was drankin' and actin' a fool, but some of our sins come back to haunt us.

"Ah guarantee you that Earlene sattin' over there missin' you just as much as you missin' her, maybe more. My granddaddy tol' me that womens act on the raw emotions that they was born with first, then they come to their right mind later. Earlene probably never meant for you to find out 'bout what she and Dyson done 'cause she was hopin' that it would never come to this. But ah'll tell you, in some small way, ah think the score been settled 'tween you and her."

Jeb sipped his coffee as he thought about the reverend's words. He tried his best to understand Earlene's justification of finding comfort in Dyson's arms – but he just couldn't. He decided that he would never understand, especially since Earlene had appeared to have nothing but contempt for Dyson as far back as he could remember.

He remembered her disapproval when Linda took up with Dyson, and how Earlene had two fits and a tantrum over the whole thing. His mind wandered over their past and all of the struggles they had endured. He always felt bad inside after he had stopped drinking because most of the tirades that he had caused were blanked out of his memory. Maybe Earlene did start to act different, but he was just too drunk to notice.

The last time he had remembered drinking was the night of Blake's birthday. It was March 24, 1929, and Blake always had a big party at his joint. Jeb faintly remembered the party at all. He remembered throwing the gin back one after the other and women dancing all around him. He would always get loose with the women in Blake's, but he never went further than a fondle and a rub here and there.

He didn't remember how he had gotten home. When he came to, he was on the front porch of the house shivering like a naked bird. He had wet his pants, and it felt like his privates were frozen solid. His head ached and he felt nauseous. Once again, he had blacked out and did God only knows what. He had lifted his head to God that morning – something that he never did. The sun was starting to peak out from beyond the clouds. He had told God that if He helped him, he would stop drinking. Jeb had confessed and accepted that he didn't have power to do it on his own, so he appealed to the Heaven that Ruthann had always said was watching.

He remembered gathering himself and tapping on the door. Earlene had slowly opened it. She had made a fire in the stove and put some coffee on. She scrambled some eggs, fried some slab bacon and green tomatoes, and made some tea biscuits. During breakfast the two of them never said a word. The girls had come to the table to eat, but they never said anything either before they headed off to school. He sipped his coffee and ate his breakfast, but he never drank alcohol again.

As Jeb sat in deep thought, Mrs. Poe walked into the kitchen.

"Good mornin'. You doin' alright?"

"I'm alright I reckon. Just doin' some thinkin' that's all."

"Well, ain't nothin' wrong with that. Do it myself sometimes."

The two of them laughed as Reverend Poe walked in.

"Mornin'. His voice was loud and robust. "Ah reckon today be a good day since ah hear some laughin' goin' on."

"Well every day be a day the Lawd has made." Mrs. Poe grinned. "Least that's what you always tell us at church honey." She grabbed the pot of coffee off the stove.

"Indeed." Reverend Poe sat down and his wife poured him some coffee. "Dyson's funeral is tomorrow mornin' and ah got to get over to the church and get thangs together. The funeral director is supposed to meet me over there at 10, so ah'll be busy today."

"Did he ever tell you if they got anybody for sure?" Mrs. Poe did ask out of concern because she was a sweet lady. She also happened to be one of Macklin's known gossips and didn't spare any details when she was telling a good story. "I mean, I hate for us to put Dyson in the ground not knowin' what really happened."

"Well, Sheriff Mann is supposed to come by, but ah don't know how much he knows. With us being the closest thing to family for Dyson, ah reckon he'll fill us in as much as he can."

Jeb didn't join in the conversation. He couldn't bring himself to discuss Dyson. The man had died a horrible death and he had been witness to the gaping holes that were left in him. He would never forget the sight of Dyson lying there in his own blood for as long as he lived, but he was also haunted by the fact that Dyson had had his daughter, *and* his wife. Dyson had a lot of money, and that money gave him privileges with women that his looks didn't. As much as Jeb tried not to care, he still wanted justice to be carried out. He thought that nobody deserved to be shot down like a dog in his own house – not even the man who had slept with his wife.

\*  \*  \*

David Moss had decided that Macklin had nothing left to offer him. When Roxy left him, she had taken the best of him with her. He loved his children, and he feared that he would never see them again. He drowned his sorrows in a bottle of gin over Christmas then went to visit his parents. Though his father wasn't too keen on seeing him, David's mother had always welcomed all of her sons with open arms. The Moss family was one of the oldest families in Macklin. Theodis Moss Sr. was the patriarch who had inherited some land from his own father. When his sons grew up, they inherited some land, as well as a little money.

Among the sons were Theodis Jr., David, Henry, Buster, and William. Three of them had left town in search of a life outside of farming in the South. David and Henry had stayed. The rumor in town was that the two of them got more money for doing so.

It was no secret that Theodis Sr. had made his way around town with the women. It was even said that he and Ms. Odessa had had a tryst some years ago. Neither one of them ever owned up to it, but the older people in town swore by God that an affair went on. Frances Moss learned quickly to turn her head from her husband's philandering ways. Her mother had told her, *If a man is bringin' his money home, ain't no use in worryin' him to death 'bout somethin' you can't control no how*. Theodis Sr. had passed his beliefs on to his sons. None of them were faithful to their wives.

David had packed a suitcase and told his parents that he was going to head to Chicago. He still had his piece of land, and had asked his father to see after it for him. He felt as if he had left his mark on Macklin in more ways than he cared to. He had numerous affairs with different women. Linda Hicks was one of them, and Viola Taylor was among one of his regulars. He had even fathered two children with her. He had known that Roxy was on to him, but he took good care of her and she had never really made a fuss until recently.

He couldn't understand why a woman got all bent out of shape when a man stepped out occasionally. His father had told him to always treat his wife with respect because the other women were just fun. The wife gets all of you, as well as all of your money, but the other woman only gets one little part. This was fine by David until Viola demanded support for her last two children. David did well financially, but Viola threatened to tell Roxy if he didn't start helping her more. He couldn't ask his father for money because his father would only blame him for not knowing how to juggle his priorities. His father would also bring up David's gambling troubles. David thought of the only other man in town who had the kind of money his father did – Dyson McCloud.

David had borrowed money from Dyson on occasion; everybody in town had. He would always pay him back, but in his own time. He had asked Dyson for $150 but Dyson had hesitated. Dyson had told him that he had a child of his own now with one on the way, and that he had to take care of them. He had told David that he would think about it and get back to him. David had agreed to wait. He couldn't do anything else.

David sat at the train station smoking a cigarette as he watched the train light in the distance. He told himself that he didn't feel guilty, but his stomach curled in knots as the train got closer to the depot. He knew that by leaving Macklin it would be that much harder to return in good standing. Sassy Flo had told him that Roxy and the children had gone to St. Louis, not to Jackson like she had told him. Sassy Flo had a sister who had moved there years before.

He would be leaving the town he had known his whole life – he had never lived anywhere but Macklin. He wouldn't even be around for Dyson's funeral, but he figured it was just as well. David Moss boarded the train and headed for Chicago.

# 27

The day of Dyson's funeral had crept up like an unexpected fever. Annie and Henry had gone back home on Christmas after the fuss had taken place. They had decided not to talk about it.

Annie had asked Henry if he loved Linda – and he had said no. He simply told Annie that opportunity had presented them both with the temptation, and they were not smart enough to turn it down. Annie made a decision to live with it because she had heard of women who had lived with worse. Lucy had stayed with Ron after he had been with Shirley Brown. Her own mother had stayed with her father after he drank and fought her. She had even heard that Ms. Erma had put up with abuse from her late husband. Over the years, women had endured a lot worse. Still, she didn't have the courage to do what Roxy did. Where would she go? Macklin was all she knew.

*     *     *

Earlene, Linda, and Ruthann had eaten dinner, practically in silence.

Emma, Linda's little girl, had played with her new doll and was oblivious to all the goings on around her. Linda's stomach had felt heavy. The guilt of what she had done had begun to consume her. She asked about Jeb, but Earlene didn't want to drudge up the whole mess, and she certainly didn't want to let Linda know what it was about.

Earlene wasn't sure how Linda would take it if she knew that her own mother had been unfaithful to her father with Dyson. How would she ever explain the attacks on Dyson's character, age, and appearance after having gone to bed with him herself? Earlene figured that if Jeb never mentioned it again, then maybe there was a chance that neither Linda nor Annie would ever have to know. But in her heart of hearts she knew Macklin too well to expect such a miracle. She was surprised that they had never heard about it before now.

Earlene had prayed for a miracle on Christmas night. She had prayed that God would touch her husband's heart and to allow forgiveness to enter. She had prayed that the two of them could mend this hole in their marriage as they had done many times over the years. She had prayed that Jeb would find his way home and back into her life. With all the craziness that had been unleashed in her family in just a few short days, she really didn't know what would come next. She really had no idea.

*       *       *

The small church was packed with grieving residents of Macklin. There was no music playing, just people humming in unison the tune of "Sweet By and By." It seemed that everyone in town had shown up, even the white Hinckley family who owned the dairy farm had come. Despite the differences that the people in town had often had with one another, when one of them died, Macklin became one big family.

A lot of people had heard that Dyson had left so much money, and many of them were anxious to know what would come of it. They sat in their seats and hummed. Some of them cried and some of them just watched. Some of them even whispered about Linda not being there because she had been arrested for killing Dyson. Millie had made it known that she believed Linda to be guilty, and she spared no one from her accusation.

Reverend Poe began the eulogy and as always the "Amens" and "go ons" resonated throughout the small place. He went on.

"Our dear brother Dyson was a good man."

"Yes!"

"He was a *hard* working man."

"Yes he was!"

"He was a man what loved to help peoples!"

"Sho nuff!" The voices got louder as Reverend Poe's eulogy started to crank up.

"Brother Dyson was jest like my own son. And he loved his daddy and stuck by him 'til the day he died."

"Yes he did!"

"And ah knowed that brother Dyson wasn't a puhfect man."

"No!"

"He wasn't the most righteous man!"

"No!"

"But he *was* a *good* man!"

The church went up in praise of Dyson McCloud. Suddenly the noise ceased as the door of the church opened. Earlene, Linda and Ruthann had walked in with Emma and baby Paul. Earlene had wanted Ruthann to stay home because she still wasn't well, but Ruthann had insisted on going to Dyson's funeral. As they stepped inside of the church, somebody shouted out.

"What she doin' here?"

It was Millie Henderson. Millie's tear stained face had turned to anger.

"Shhhh," Somebody yelled out. "This ain't the place."

"This *is* the place. She ain't got no business being here."

Stunned, Reverend Poe had stopped speaking. He looked out at the crowd, and before he could utter another word, Ms. Erma had yelled out.

"Now wait a minute! This is still the house of the Lawd, not to mention a man's funeral. And yall need to show some respect, or at least the 'lil bit of decency you was born with!"

"Aw hush woman, you yellin' too!" Margaret Jessup's voice rang out. "You and that slack-jawed friend of yourn Ms. Odessa probably behind all of this here mess anyhow!"

"Now wait a minute!" Ms. Odessa chimed in. "Don't you dare drag mah name in this. You jest still mad 'cause that two-timin' husband of yourn is dodging fire-balls in the devah's hell!"

"That be enough!" Reverend Poe's voice was like thunder. "Everybody jest calm down rett now!"

Silence fell over the congregation. The reverend continued.

"Ain't nary one o' you gat a heaven or hell to put nobody in. God gat the last say over every one of us. Ah ain't gonna let yall stand up here fussin' and carryin' on in the presence of the dead. Let this man rest in peace!"

"I didn't kill him!" Linda ran to the front, the breeze from her body seemed to plant everybody's feet to the floor. "But I might as well have done it. I did him wrong."

"Gal sat down!" Earlene pleaded.

"Naw mama." Linda's voice cracked as she stood in front of the congregation with every eye on her. "I ain't never shot a gun a day in my life. My daddy tried to teach me and my sister when we was little, but I wouldn't go near a gun."

"Gal sat down! You ain't got to explain nothin' to these folks." Earlene snatched at Linda's arm with one hand, as she held Paul with the other. She led her back to her seat.

"What about you Earlene? Don't you need to explain to your dawta how you and Dyson was…"

"That's it. I don't have to stay here for this. Linda, let's go."

Earlene and Linda walked out of the church, and half the crowd followed behind them.

"Tell them Earlene, 'bout how you asked me to cover for you when you was meetin' Dyson in the afternoons when them gals was little. The noise that you and Dyson was makin', hmph, I didn't ever thank you would go back to bed with your own husband."

Earlene turned around to see who was speaking. It was Laney Grilson, a woman whom she had once considered a friend. Laney had lived next door to Dyson for years. Earlene soon realized that it was a huge mistake to confide in her – though she was never too sure until that night at Ms. Odessa's house when Roxy Hicks and Viola Taylor had confirmed it. No information was ever privileged in Macklin.

"Laney, I ain't gonna stand here and let you insult me another minute! My mama always said be careful who you call friend, and you sho ain't no friend o' mine you loud mouth heffah!" Earlene stormed toward the door of the church leaving Linda standing in the middle of the aisle.

"Mama, wait. What she talkin about?" Linda yelled toward Earlene's back. "Is what she talkin about true?"

"Yes it's true," Laney walked toward Linda. "Ya mama had such a problem with you and Dyson cuz she wanted him for her own self. That's why she acted like he was the dirt under her feets all them years, cuz she didn't want you and nobody else to have him after she did. That's why yo daddy run off and left her, cuz he fount out that she ain't nothin' but a two-bit hussy!"

"That's it!" Reverend Poe's voice seemed to shake the frame of the church. "Enough is enough and too much stanks! If yall didn't come here to pay respects to Dyson, then yall can jest leave this church. Ah don't like what you talkin' bout one bit, and ah sho know that the Lawd don't like it either."

To Reverend Poe's surprise, everybody in the church got up and headed toward the door. As always, Ruthann had kept quiet until the right moment came for her to speak. The crowd had filed out of the doors of the small church with the exception of the two deacons who stood watch over Dyson's casket.

There were whispers and outright shouts of judgment and blame. Babies cried, old mothers moaned, and the young women wept. The men in the midst kept their composure as they usually did during such chaos in Macklin.

As the crowd began to get out of hand with blasphemies and the like, Jeb was spotted coming up the road. He had stayed behind when Reverend Poe and his wife left for the funeral earlier that morning, but decided that he couldn't stay away after all.

Ruthann moved her way out from the crowd and waited for Jeb to reach the mass of people standing behind her. She held herself up with a cane, her back seeming to give way right there as she stood. Jeb reached the crowd and silence engulfed the crowd.

Jeb began to speak. "I…"

"Just you wait a minute Jeb." Ruthann interrupted. "I thank enough non-sense done been said here today." She turned around and looked into the faces of everybody there; most of them she had washed right from their mothers' wombs. She began to remember that Heaven's Eyes had been there for each birth, and they had also witnessed every moment in Macklin. Those eyes were watching even now. As she spoke, the people of Macklin, Mississippi began to remember also.

"It grieves mah heart to know that this town done come to such a thang. Why if the Reverend wasn't standin' right here ah would tell all of yall somethin' nuther. Bless his heart cause he the only one in this whole town ever act like he had more since that God give a grasshopper.

"Seem like ever since Shirley Brown come through here some 20 years ago this town ain't been the same. Yall mens lost your minds and ain't fount 'em since. You womens don't do nothin' but run one nuther down and stay hauled up in some mess – all the time! You oughta be thankin' bout these chilluns you ain't tryin' to raise and the generations that's gonna come behind them. Ah feel sorry for these next generations. Folks supposed to feel proud of what they come from. Sometimes ah can't hardly believe that ah toiled all them years for them white folks as a slave, working my fingers to the bone – and mah mama before me

– kissin' up and smilin' round the big house in them white folks faces jest to keep from dyin.

"When the good Lawd set us free, ah jest knowed that we was gonna be a better race o' peoples jest cause we was grateful and knowed what it been like to live hell on this here earth, but it seem like the farther away from 'mancipation we got, the crazier we got. Here we are at a man's funeral and folks is shoutin' at one nuther cross the Lawd's house.

"Not only that, but this man stretched out yonder didn't deserve to go the way he did – but it done. May the Lawd have mercy on the soul what shot him full of holes. The Lawd is lookin' at that man right now – that's right – twas a man what killed Dyson – not Linda. Lawd do know that she ain't innocent, sattin' here with not one but *two* babies by her own sister's husband.

"Heaven's eyes is always watchin' and Heaven knows and tells me all its secrets. Heaven knows jest who kilt Dyson – jest like ah know."

Ruthann's words always had the uncanny ability to put people into a  trance like state. No one moved; maybe out of respect, but more likely out of fear. Ruthann slowly turned and scanned each face; her eyes now glossed over with cataracts appeared cold and dark blue. She spoke again, only this time her voice was not as commanding.

"All of yall so quick to shove a finger at one nuther and Lawd knows ain't nary one of you innocent. My own family done did some thangs ah ain't proud of, but ah wants you all to thank twice when you get as ole as ah am now, and your own grandchillun carryin' on worse than this. Before you go judgin' them and pointin' fingers – jest remember this day."

As Ruthann finished, people stood still and no one had said a word.

Reverend Poe was in tears as he headed back into the church and told the deacons to close up the casket.

"We gonna go and bury this man now right next to his daddy." The two deacons and the funeral director shook their heads in unison.

"Ah'm gonna get a few of these men out here to help us out." Reverend Poe's voice had been reduced to just above a whisper. "His daddy would have been proud of how Dyson kept his land up all these years."

*     *     *

Eddie rushed through the streets of downtown Chicago. He had a gig and he was late for rehearsal with the band. In his rush to get to the Night Owl, he thought his eyes had played a trick on him. They had been known to play tricks on him in the past, especially the time he thought he had seen his dead grandfather sitting in the audience of the club one night as he played. Surely his eyes had betrayed him when he had seen a white man tip his hat to him as he stepped out of the ballroom of the Drake Hotel after playing for a wedding. Now, once again, his eyes had to be playing the cruelest of jokes. Eddie slowed down as the man he saw moved closer to him.

At first Eddie wasn't sure, but the closer the man got to him, he had become certain. This man was indeed Dyson McCloud; he was sure that was the name on the piece of paper that the waitress had written down that day in that little spot called Blake's in Macklin. This was the man he had seen when he was perched behind the tree on the man's land. This was the man who had fathered Linda's children.  As their eyes met in passing, Eddie was sure beyond a doubt that this was the tall, somewhat handsome man that he had watched from afar.  This was the man he had almost confronted on his last day in Macklin, Mississippi.

Eddie knew that this Dyson couldn't have known who he was because he had never seen him.  Eddie wondered immediately if Linda was in town too.  The very thought nearly forced him to turn around and catch up with this Dyson to ask if he and Linda had come to Chicago together but Eddie knew better.  He decided to keep walking and not be any later for rehearsal than he already was.  As he neared the Night Owl, he did wonder; *why had Dyson McCloud come to Chicago?*

After arriving in Chicago, David checked into the Canterbury Hotel on 12th and Ashland.  He had been caught up in the mad afternoon rush after he left the train station.  He had decided to stay in Chicago and try his best to forget about Macklin.  It would be hard, but he would have to forget about Roxy and the children too.  The hotel lobby was full of people as he made his way to the front desk to sign the registry.

"You have to get to the back of the line."  A white man with white hair and a mustache just as white, said to him.

"But there ain't… I mean… no one is standing here sir." David obliged the man.  He knew he wasn't in the south anymore, but the man's outburst reminded him that he was still out of his comfort zone.

"Don't you see all of these people walking around you?  You have to wait until this area is clear, just in case somebody else wants to check in."

David stepped back and waited like he was told. The men in suits walked out of the door of the hotel. The man behind the desk spoke up. "Now you can come on up."

David grabbed the registry and signed in: *Daniel Moore.*

\*　　\*　　\*

Annie's great-grandchildren continued to sing and play in the front yard. They had been her world since the first grandchild had been born. Hester had made Annie a grandmother on her $42^{nd}$ birthday – a little boy, whom Hester and her husband had named Henry, since Annie never did name one of their children for him. The years seemed to melt away after that. Annie had felt betrayed by Henry for years after she had found out about him and Linda. At the time she was pregnant with their fourth child; a boy they named Thomas. Sadie and Ruthie had come after that.

Since Linda had come back to Macklin that summer day, Annie's life had changed. After Dyson's funeral, people in Macklin began to change also. Annie's father returned home to Earlene. Ruthann had died in her sleep one week later, and Linda had moved away to Memphis. Linda had left Emma and Paul behind, and since they had been Henry's children, Annie had taken them both in and raised them as her own.

Somehow, she had learned to accept what Henry and Linda had done and found peace every time she looked at the children. Henry seemed to love her even more after they had taken the children in; maybe it was his guilt, she had thought, or maybe he had finally come to believe in the sanctity of marriage – something that no Moss man had ever done. As Paul grew older, the more he looked like

Henry. Annie was sure that even though Isaiah was her and Henry's child, it was Paul who took it the hardest when Henry died of heart failure at the age of thirty-eight. Paul was only six years old, and he was never quite the same after that.

It was kind of odd to Annie, but after Dyson's funeral, no one ever spoke of Earlene and Dyson, Linda and Henry, or any other alleged affair in town. Shirley Brown's name had also become a faint memory in the minds of the people in Macklin.

As Annie sat there rocking in her chair, she thought of those days and how they seemed to drag on forever. She thought about the last day Ruthann had been alive and how she had spoken of sowing and reaping. She had given her last spill about "Heaven's Eyes Watching," and that the man who had killed Dyson would pay. She had also said that all her life she had hoped to live to see the day when color wouldn't matter, but she looked at her great-great-grandchildren and said, *I don't know if they will ever live to see that day either*.

Millie Henderson went back to her life in Little Rock. Ms. Odessa and Ms. Erma lived out their days in Macklin, as did Earlene and Jeb, and Lucy and Ron. Reverend Poe and his wife took over Dyson's land and the rest of Dyson's money, which came to fifty seven thousand dollars. Dyson had planned to leave Macklin quietly in the night, but he was stopped in his tracks by a shotgun in his own kitchen.

Linda lived in Memphis for a while and eventually Little Rock before moving to New York City. She married a white man named Edward Rowen. They had a son who became one of the first Black men to own a law firm in the city of New York. Linda lived to see the only grandchild she knew of – a girl whom her son and his wife named Annie. Linda died shortly after that at the age of sixty two.

Roxy Moss had indeed moved to St. Louis. She married a doctor and had two more children. It was rumored that she had plotted revenge on David for the flings that he had had around Macklin. No one knew for sure, but it was certain that he had met a terrible fate. He was found dead in an alley in Chicago with ID in his jacket pocket with the name Daniel Moore on it. It was a mystery to most everybody who knew him, but Annie had remembered Ruthann talking about reaping and sowing. Yes, Annie knew that *Heaven's Eyes* were watching and that they always would be.

## *About the Author:*

Jacqueline J. Andrews was born and raised in Chicago, Illinois. She received a B.A. in Business Education and an MFA in Creative Writing from Chicago State University. She teaches English Composition, Creative Writing, and Studies in Literary Genres for several colleges and universities.

In her free time, she loves to read, travel, and shop. She also likes trying new restaurants and different cuisines all around the world. She currently resides in a suburb of Chicago with her husband.

## *Note from the Author:*

Thank you for reading the book to the end. I really appreciate your support. If you like what you have read or want to learn more about me or the town of Macklin, please visit any of the Websites below.